To my friend
Buddy,

Enjoy Louisa
and learn from
her

17 February 2007

Richard

LOUISA

Richard Emmel

Parson Place Press
Mobile, Alabama

Copyright © 2007 by Richard Emmel
All rights reserved.

All Scripture quotations are taken from the King James Authorized Version of the *Holy Bible*.

ISBN 10: 0-9786567-0-9
ISBN 13: 978-0-9786567-0-6

Library of Congress Control Number: 2007920080

This first novel is dedicated to Andrew Emmel, our precious, youngest son, who died too early. In his brief twenty years, he taught us how to live, and we shall be forever thankful.

Contents

Chapter 1—An Overview 7
Chapter 2–How a Child of Africa Became
   an American Slave 13
Chapter 3—Servitude and a Surprise 25
Chapter 4—Fifteen Years of Learning
   While Performing Slave Labor 36
Chapter 5—A Blessed Slave 48
Chapter 6—Becoming a Woman 63
Chapter 7—Heaven Help Us 69
Chapter 8—Teaching Prejudice 75
Chapter 9—Free at Last 81
Chapter 10–Two Unforgettable Events 95
Chapter 11–Becoming a Mother 113
Chapter 12—A Friend in Braintree 121
Chapter 13–Happiness Taken 136
Chapter 14—On Our Own 141
Chapter 15—A New Beginning 150
Chapter 16–Our First Article 158
Chapter 17—The First Column 167
Chapter 18—The Improbable Dream 181

Recollecting My Life

Memory, immortal pow'r, I trace thy spring:
Uplift my strains, while I thy glory fling:
The acts of long departed years, by thee
Recover'd, in due order rang'd we flee:
Thy pow'r the long-forgotten calls from night,
That sweetly plays before the fancy's flight.

Phillis Wheatley

Chapter 1—An Overview

God made me smart. I learn things quickly, write well, and enjoy thoughts about the future. Being a slave, I could not enjoy my gifts, but had to practice much self-control, lest I was considered smart. White people punished slaves who acted the least little bit smart, sometimes even killing them. I could never say what I thought, for fear of insulting white people. The only time I could relax was when I was with other slaves. As a house servant, there was seldom a time I was not around white people. Working in the big house had many advantages, but a big disadvantage was keeping a respectful silence at all times when on duty, typically eighteen hours straight. I longed for the day when I would be free to talk. In my bones, I knew the good Lord would someday grant me freedom. Until that day, I had to work hard at being common and not draw attention to myself.

I learned this lesson early. As a young slave, I waited on my master's twins during their tutoring sessions. I wanted so much to play with them rather than stand around waiting on them hand and foot. Mary and Nathaniel Wheatley were my age. Mary was sickly, and everyone pampered her, but Nathaniel was a healthy and mischievous boy whose personal magnetism endeared him to all who knew him—even me. I say "even me" because I saw how he abused other slaves, but never me. I am sure my relationship with his mother had something to do with the fact he never mistreated me. Although they were my contemporaries, they were never my playmates; I was their servant, and so I had to hide my thoughts and problems while at the same time showing concern for them. Oh, how I wanted just a little attention and the soothing hand of a caregiver.

I wanted to learn and craved the opportunities they so took for granted. My soul longed for the instruction that the twins disregarded. As I sat behind the twins and listened intently to the schoolmaster's lessons, they bedeviled the poor man with nonsense questions. Most annoying was their habit of asking me for a drink just when he was about to make an important point. Not only did I have to leave the room's wisdom, but I also had to leave what I can only describe as a delightful stupor brought about by the allure of knowledge.

Although I doubt they deliberately made me miss the instruction, I could never be sure. To keep us constantly in place, whites routinely abused us. That aspect of life never ceased, even after I became free. The color of my skin has always dictated my status on this earth and kept me socially enslaved. There were some people, like Mr. Franklin, who thought highly of me. The good people of England also cared for me. Loyalty to my second family brought me back to America, even though I could have easily remained in Britain. I got that loyalty from my African family—my real family. The beliefs of my father and mother were so much a part of me that I returned to enslavement rather than stay where I enjoyed freedom and respect.

I dream about seeing my father and mother again, but hold out little hope for that happening. I was only with them seven years, but they still have a powerful influence on me. I will write about my early training in the African bush to dispel the attitude that Africa is a country of savages. I have seen more savagery in America than I ever did in Africa. My father was the chief of a large tribe, so I knew what happened both in my village and the surrounding area. Just because my people are primitive does not mean we are savages. I would like to see a Bostonian make an elaborate costume from just leaves, light wood, shells, and feathers, but my people could easily live in Boston. I am getting away from my story, but I promise another book about Mother Africa.

I arrived in Boston in the spring of 1760 as a frail little African girl who was the last bit of cargo sold by a cruel slaver. The brutality of the three-month voyage from Africa left me broken in both body and spirit and very nearly dead. The slave ship captain would likely have dumped me in the harbor if John and Susannah Wheatley hadn't bought me for a few shillings. For having saved my life, such as it was, I suppose I owe the Wheatleys something.

When the slave catchers took me, I lost everything and everyone—my parents, my brother, my home, my identity. By the time they packed me aboard the slave ship, I felt nothing but despair, and it wasn't long before I saw that despair in others, too. While at sea, it was a rare thing for the captured Africans to be brought up on deck, but when the slavers did so—to wash us down and air out the hold—some of our number jumped over the side and into the endless sea. A sure death in the ocean was better than a filthy life below the deck.

As I write this, I don't know my exact age. My life in America began the day Susannah Wheatley gambled on my potential as a house servant. She thought that with just a little food and care, I might live, and if I didn't, she would have lost only five shillings, less than the cost of a dress in her husband's dry goods store. I think I am twenty-nine years old now, but I could be as young as twenty-seven or as old as thirty-one. Slaves rarely know their age, because we have no birth records. My master has birth records for his livestock, but not for his slaves. As far as a slave-owner is concerned, a slave has no past. For a slave, only today and tomorrow matter, and for me, the bleak future robbed me of my tomorrows.

I am talking about the block of time from my arrival until I was freed. Every day I knew my life could be taken for an action thought of as being inconsiderate by a white person. Yes, it could be any white person, not just my master or mistress. I saw harsh physical punishment and death meted out to slaves for false reasons. I never could adjust to the abuse I saw. Trying not to be mistreated was a daily challenge that took much energy and effort. It made me tense, but I had to appear friendly and respectful. Knowing that I could be hurt by any white person kept me fearful, even after I got my freedom. It is yet another unseen scar of slavery.

As you will read, I spent fifteen years as a slave for the Wheatley family. Mrs. Wheatley remained true to her word and released me on her death. My last few years as a slave were awkward, because I had become a well-known writer, yet I continued my enslavement. My British friends did not understand how the Wheatleys could continue ownership of me. Mrs. Wheatley was ill during my entire servitude. Many times during my fifteen years with the family, Mrs. Wheatley was near death, so I was used to it. I had to return to Boston when I got word that she was on her deathbed, but I fully expected her to pull through, as she had done so many times before. As much as I wanted my freedom, I could not bear to think about the cost—the death of my mistress and best friend.

The illness that enslaved Mrs. Wheatley was a much harsher master than were my owners. She regularly let me know that sharing books with me brought enthusiasm to her life. When I wrote my first poem, she called me a genius and told me that I had a special gift. At her death, a new life began for me.

Guessing my age to be a young twenty when freedom came, I immediately married a strong, intelligent African. Also, I soon became quite ill and thought that I would have but a brief taste of freedom before death took me.

Influenza moved through Boston, taking many people who were too weak to fight its deadly grip. I was still very weak and felt as if the time for my eternal pilgrimage would be soon. As dreadful as the thought of death was at such an early age, for the first time since coming to America, I felt free. It was our misfortune that our first son was a breach birth. The midwife was unable to move him properly, turning our happiness into grief. I recovered from influenza, but will never recover from my little boy's death.

Just a year later, and this time not cursed by sickness, I am again close to the miracle of birth. Yet, I know my body still bears the scars of slavery that could keep us childless. Not any richer, we must depend on the skills of the same midwife who was there at the birth and death of our first child. I pray that the Lord will take my life this time and spare the precious child inside of me.

Perhaps the reader is wondering what I meant when I wrote "the scars of slavery could keep me childless." I had a sickness when I first arrived that made me very weak and filled my lungs with vile mucus. I do not know if that affected other parts of my body. Also, I was abused while being held captive at Boston Harbor. I will write no more, because I do not want the ugly facts to sully this book. Like a bird on a perch, I seek balance. It would be easy for me to write about the unthinkable, because it was part of being a slave in America, but I also know the good America. In this book, I have chosen to write mostly about the good America. I faced this issue when slaves began to rebel. Should I revolt or continue serving the Wheatleys? I balanced things by writing rebellious lines in my poetry, while continuing to be the good servant.

I remember looking up at the night sky and thinking that death would take away all shackles and unite me with my little boy whom the Lord called so early. Now, near my ninth month, I realize that my second child may join his brother in heaven. This I keep to myself, so as not to cause my husband, John Peters, any more grief than he has already endured.

In the hope that our child may be spared the fate of his brother, I write my life's story, so that he will know his mother and what I and so many other slaves struggled to accomplish. By the grace of God, my child and this story will survive.

I have waited until now to write, because writing about myself is difficult. It is easier to write about other people. People consider me a good writer, but perhaps that is because I describe the subjects of my writing not as they are, but as they should be. I do not want that to happen with my own story. I want my son to know the truth.

Who better to write the story of a slave but a slave? Certainly, no white man could do so. After all, who would read such a thing? Most slaves are not permitted to read. When we die, our owners don't honor our memories; they give no more thought to our passing than they would to the loss of a worn-out shoe. No, I must write my story and trust in Providence that someday it will be published.

"To the Right Honourable William, Earl of Dartmouth, His Majesty's Principal Secretary of State for North America"

> I, young in life, by seeming cruel fate
> Was snatched from Afric's fanc'd happy seat:
> What pangs excruciating must molest,
> What sorrows labour in my Parent's breast?
>
> Phillis Wheatley

Chapter 2—How a Child of Africa Became an American Slave

My real name is not Louisa Wheatley. It is Farih Morowa, daughter of Bewnu, chief of the Fulani. The best translation of my name into English is "Gifted with Imagination." My masters changed it. They saw it as their right to do so, for they owned me. Mr. Wheatley bought me because he wanted a household slave to tend to his ailing wife. He responded to a slave ship owner's newspaper advertisement that offered young females as part of a cargo of human beings abducted from Senegal on the west coast of Africa and transported across the ocean to the New World.

Slave traders frequented Senegal, not so much for its favorable location, but because the traits of its people made it the slave center of the world. Senegal men were smart and strong, and their trusting nature made them easy prey for the slave catchers. The river made it easy to get and take away our strong young men and women. The old and the young were often slaughtered. A few escaped.

I was not a Senegali, although my village, Rosso, was on the banks of the Senegal River. I was of the Fulani people—targets of the slavers when they couldn't fill their ships with Senegali men. My father, Bewnu, was a noble and wise Fulani chief, revered among our people as a peacemaker. Rather than fight territorial battles, he prevented wars by negotiating fair boundaries with other tribes. He gained the respect of everyone, because he took the time to learn and speak the languages of many tribes. Even if he did not know the language, he could talk by gesture and facial expression.

I must hold on to my past. One day stands out for me. It was the day before my capture when my father won over the chief of a warring band by making signs in the dust. What my father did kept our village from being attacked. He and I were checking the community garden when he sensed danger. My father knew something was wrong. Without scaring me, he tried to get me to go back to the safety of the main lodge, but I was enjoying the garden inspection too much and would not leave.

Without any warning, every village gate was surrounded by men wearing leopard skins and waving long spears and bows. I was so scared my legs were shaking, making it very difficult for me to stand. A very funny-sounding voice came from my mouth asking my father what was happening. He told me once more, soothingly, to run to the main lodge, but I would not leave his side. He could not get rid of me, so he had to risk both our lives to keep our village safe.

As I think back on this incident, I hate the fact that I caused my father so much more trouble, but I am glad that I witnessed firsthand his ability to solve what seemed like an impossible situation. We had well-trained warriors to defend us, but many Fulani would have died in the battle. With one command, my father could have unleashed enough killing power to easily take out all the leopard people, but he risked his life and mine when he walked, unarmed, straight to the invading chief.

There is no telling how much turmoil I caused my father by refusing to leave his side. I was captured the next day, and we never got to talk about what happened. Knowing my father, I am sure he would not have told anyone that his beloved daughter was a nuisance and could have caused us both to die.

My father, our chief, drew two people putting up a main pole in the dust as the invading chief watched. The invader understood that the drawing meant people working together to make shelter. My father then drew a line from one of the drawings to himself. From the other drawing he drew a line to the invader, and it was understood the drawings were the two chiefs.

The dusty ground became a huge tablet on which each man drew. My father found out that the invading tribe had been attacked by slavers who killed or took all but the people surrounding our village. People from an unknown land armed with weapons we had never seen before and could not combat were capturing African adults and killing the young and old. They were moving down our river, taking village after village.

The two chiefs agreed to a peace that kept both tribes safe. It was also agreed that both tribes would merge and move as fast as possible away from the river to the large lake far away. This meant we would have to abandon our beautiful village and live like nomads. It would take two days to make preparations for our forced march to the safety of the great jungle.

My birthday was the next day, and I was both sad and glad to spend it in our village. I planned to get up early to fish in our river, because soon I would no longer be able to sit on its comforting banks. My beautiful river served as the road to our village, a road now used by the horrible slavers to steal our people. The plans were to burn my birthplace to the ground, so that the slavers would think no village ever existed there, and a wildfire had simply burned part of the forest. There would be people covering our trail as we moved into the jungle, wiping out all traces of our existence. As I write this, I know my father took both tribes so deep into Mother Africa that no slaver would have taken the trouble to find them. Yes, I know they must be safe, but now I will tell you more of what I remember about my village.

Only accidents caused the spilling of Fulani blood in our village, usually from the boys' initiation rites. The boys would fight pretend battles, and their clubs were supposed to miss their targets, but sometimes the boys would get carried away. Such is the way with boys. My own brother was wounded in that way and required five stitches. The doctor pulled a hair from an animal's tail, boiled it, and, using a fish bone as a needle, put five stitches in a deep cut above his right eye. My brother was very proud of the small scar left behind.

Wounds like my brother's reminded us of the battles fought before my father became chief of the Fulani. Under my father's leadership, our tribe foreswore war and became artisans; we maintained only those few warriors who were needed for defense against slavers, but such precautions were not always enough.

The slavers captured me on my birthday. I arose early, as I had planned, and went fishing in the river. My brother had caught the fish for his birthday meal, and I wanted to match his feat. The sun was just coming from the other side of the world, and my cork float was barely visible in the dim light of dawn. It was two weeks into the rainy season, and the river was twice its normal size. I never saw or heard the small boat that docked just downriver from where I sat.

A large man—a stranger from another tribe—appeared behind me. I was startled, but not afraid. He tried to talk with me, but, unlike my father, I couldn't speak his language, and he could not speak mine. Although he was an African man, he wore strange clothing. Without warning, he threw me to the ground, forced open my mouth, and stuffed something inside that almost choked me. He tied my hands behind my back, and then bound my hands to my ankles so I could only kneel or lie on my side like a strung bow. He forced me into his boat, and then guided it into the current. As he navigated, he kept me pinned to the floor with his boot.

The rope ate through the flesh of my wrists and ankles, cutting off the circulation to my hands and feet, causing them to swell. I tried to flex my body enough to relieve the pain, but when my muscles relaxed, the rope only cut deeper into my flesh. Only moments before, I had been a respected member of the Fulani—the chief's daughter; now, I was little more than my kidnapper's footrest.

I must have fainted at some point. I have no memory of my boat ride into slavery. When I awoke, my ropes had been retied, enabling me to sit upright, but they were still unbearably tight. To this day, callused scars encircle my wrists and ankles; the scarf I always wear around my neck conceals the remnants of an ugly rope burn.

During the trip downriver, I survived on scraps from my captor's meals, and quenched my thirst by licking brackish water from the bottom of the boat. Mostly, I was in a stupor; I begged the Spirit for a merciful death.

The little riverboat maneuvered alongside a crowded dock. As my kidnapper tied up the boat, he spat upon me. Although I had a sense of why he had taken me—we had been warned about the slave catchers—I had no understanding of the reason for his contempt. He hauled me out of the boat and tied me to a post. I was nothing more than a small parcel of goods to him, but, as much as I hated and feared him, I sensed that my safety—perhaps even my survival—depended on him. When he disappeared inside a large building, I lost my balance and fell to the ground, writhing like a tethered snake.

I fell, because I was so very hungry and thirsty, and because fear took away all control. I can still see in my mind the imprint in the dust much like that of the snake killed on a dusty trail. As my head began to clear, I sensed that I was at the mercy of my despicable captor. I had to hope that the brief time I had been around this man was enough for him to care about me. Even if his care was nothing more than one might have for a trapped insect, it was my only chance to live. I was his only catch, so perhaps he would not let the slavers do the easier thing and just get rid of me. As my head cleared, the will to live swelled up inside me.

Eventually, I regained my composure and managed to stand up and lean against the pole. Others like me were tied to poles, but most of the captives—men, women, and children—were held in cages, shackled with ropes and chains. I was one of the few with clothes on my back. Soon, another slave catcher came along and tied a boy about my brother's age to my pole. After the slave catcher left, the boy stood quietly for a few moments and then began to rant. He chewed at his ropes and yelled out a word that sounded like "father." Another man came by and tried to stop him, but the boy had already chewed through the ropes on his wrists and was untying the ropes around his ankles.

Suddenly, there was an explosion. Pungent smoke filled the air. Until then, I had never seen a gun or heard one discharge, but when the smoke cleared, I realized that the man had shot the boy in the head. The boy bounced against the pole and slid to the ground, motionless. Blood poured from his wound and formed a rivulet that pooled at my feet. I heard him gasp one last "father," and then he died. A little while later, some other men came by with a cart and heaped the boy's body onto a stack of other corpses.

The man who stole me from my family reappeared with another man. They came to my pole and examined me in the same way that my father examined livestock. The men were impressed by my perfect teeth, but dismayed by my small stature. I heard my captor's name, Beheidi, spoken for the first time as he argued with the other man. He wanted more money for me than the man was willing to pay. Finally, Beheidi accepted two pieces of gold, but he cursed the buyer. I forced a smile in an awkward attempt to appease Beheidi as he walked past me, but it was a mistake. Beheidi mistook my smile for mockery, and he slapped me so hard that he broke one of my front teeth. My face stung from his blow, but the exposed nerve of my tooth sent hot pain streaming through my head.

Later, I discovered that the man who bought me from Beheidi was the captain of a slave ship. Captain Gwin dragged me to another boat dock by way of a rocky path. The rocks cut my feet, and I lagged behind, but Captain Gwin forced me to keep walking, or be dragged over the rocks. As we approached Captain Gwin's ship, we waded along the shore of what appeared to me as an endless lake. The water was salty, and it stung the wounds on my ankles. The captain pulled me to the beach and put me in a wooden trough filled with the same salty water. He scrubbed my body vigorously with a long-handled brush, and then, satisfied that I was clean, he put me into a cage along with several young men—all of them were, like me, now slaves.

For three days, I was beset by anguish and confusion. I felt like the animal my new masters treated me like. Our captors fed us mush in a grimy trough and water in dirty pots. We ate from the trough like pigs because our hands were always bound; we lapped water like dogs for the same reason.

The cage was narrow and tight. As I was smaller than the others, I had little difficulty standing, but most of the captives couldn't do so because the roof of the cage was too low. By the third day, there were fifteen people in the cage—three women and twelve men. We were so tightly packed that we couldn't lie down, so we slept by leaning against the wall or against one another. We performed our bodily functions in a kettle set in one corner; soon, it overflowed with excrement.

The three days I spent in the cage were comfortable compared with the next three months I spent in total darkness in the hold of the slave ship. The mere thought of that journey stills my heart and my mind, filling me with the memory of pain and death.

In the middle of my third day in the cage, the slavers removed us, shackled our ankles together and marched us aboard Captain Gwin's ship, the *Louisa*. The crewmen packed eighty-four of us in the cargo hold, chained together so tightly that the adults couldn't stretch out their full length. Many years later, I learned that the *Louisa* normally packed a hundred and twenty-four slaves at the outset of a voyage. I can't begin to conceive how tightly packed we would have been had there been forty more bodies with us. Even so, the *Louisa* arrived at Boston bearing only seventy slaves. The crew dispatched fourteen of our number overboard during the voyage, some of them while they were still alive. The slavers disposed of the sick along with the dead, because it was more profitable for them to collect the insurance proceeds on a dead slave than risk a low sale price on a sick one.

Because they expected slaves to die en route, slave captains customarily packed more slaves than their ships could comfortably hold, but once aboard ship, the captains rarely inspected their cargo in person, and so they didn't see the misery this custom produced. Even if they had done so, I doubt that they would have cared; to most of these pious men, there was no evil in their profession. Rather, they were considered sharp businessmen—they were called "tight packers"—and greatly respected for their ability to transport large numbers of slaves across the ocean, even though many of their human cargo died on the way. The truth was that "loose packers" started their voyages with fewer slaves, but often arrived with more and healthier slaves than did the tight packers.

The shipboard overseers appointed two slaves to dispose of the dead along with the garbage and the excrement. The slaves eagerly vied for the privilege of carrying out this task because it afforded them the opportunity to go above decks for fresh air and earn a few extra morsels of food. The rest of us gasped below and survived on watery swill that the crewmen poured unceremoniously onto the floor. Because I was so small and weak, the slaves chained to either side of me licked up most of my food. Chewing on wood and eating straw helped quiet the pain of starvation.

Just before we reached Boston, five sick slaves were drowned. Coming so close to survival made their deaths especially hard to bear. The slavers waited this late, I suppose, thinking the five might regain enough strength to be sold, but Captain Gwin didn't want potential buyers to think that he was offering unfit slaves for sale, so he had the four men and one woman thrown overboard with the garbage. He touted the excellent conditions aboard his ship as the reason for such a healthy cargo.

The day before we reached port, the crew brought ten slaves at a time up from below to be cleansed of excrement and vomit. This was the first bath and the first glimpse of daylight I had had in three months, and I was momentarily blinded by the sunlight. After we had all been scrubbed clean, the crew flushed out the hold while we stood shivering on deck. The crew chief inspected each of us. Any slave with an unsightly sore or even a sickly look could be thrown overboard; even the presence of one unhealthy slave might lower the price of the entire cargo.

Late that night, the crew inspected us one more time. They gave each of us loincloths and returned us to the cargo hold. Although the hold had been washed, its stench remained.

Upon reaching port, the crew led us in chains to holding pens on the docks. There, we were given solid food for the first time in three months. Many of us had a difficult time digesting it. We remained in the holding pens for several days, all the while eating solid food and sleeping, at long last, on straw mats.

The day of the slave auction came. The adult men were sold first, followed by the adult women, and then the children. I was one of the last slaves put on the block, and Mr. Wheatley was one of only three men who bid on me. I later learned that he bought me for five shillings.

A crewman from the *Louisa* unchained me, and one of Mr. Wheatley's servants led me to the Wheatley carriage. Although I couldn't understand her, she spoke, pointing to herself, and saying, "Chloe" which I took to be her name. I pointed to myself, and said, "Farih Morowa," but Chloe only shook her head sadly and uttered more words I couldn't understand.

The Wheatleys had brought some old clothing, but nothing suitable for a small girl. Chloe helped me into an old dress that was much too big for me, making me look even smaller than I was. She pointed to the back seat of the buggy, and I climbed aboard.

She spoke to me again, but I understood only her angry tone. She pointed to herself again and said, "Miss Chloe." I nodded in response. I smiled, trying to make friends, and again pointed to myself. "Farih Morowa," I said.

Miss Chloe shook her head. She looked over at the stern of the slave ship and then pointed to me. "Louisa. Louisa Wheatley." She shook her head again. "No more Farih Morowa. Louisa. Louisa Wheatley."

Mr. Wheatley drove the carriage through the streets of Boston. Everything appeared very strange to me. I had never seen so many buildings so close together. It seemed to me that there were more people there than in all of Africa. Mr. Wheatley's house was very big—it could have housed half the people in my village!

It was difficult for me to understand how anyone could make such a tall, strong building. The Wheatley house was as tall as a tree and was made from square red stones. In my village, we made our homes and storehouses from poles and thatch. The red earth was our floor and the buildings were far apart. It was a long time before I understood how grey mud could harden between bricks and create a wall as high as a tree.

The Wheatley home had polished wooden floors and high ceilings. On the walls were painted images of the Wheatley family members. They were so lifelike that I felt that they were staring at me, and I had never seen so much furniture.

Miss Chloe helped me settle into my new quarters—a small room on the first floor of the house. Despite its size and sparse furnishings, it was paradise compared with the hold of the slave ship and, although I had yet to learn the nature of my duties or the restrictions of my station in the household, I took the relative comfort of my new quarters as a good sign.

I solved the communication problem with Chloe by using sign language. Chloe and I managed my bath, and then she outfitted me in appropriate clothes and gave me a meal before introducing me to the Wheatley household. Late that night, alone on the rough cot that served as my bed, my thoughts returned to my family back in Rosso, and I shed silent, bitter tears at the thought of having lost them forever.

*In God have I put my trust:
I will not be afraid what man can do unto me.*

Psalm 56:11

Chapter 3—Servitude and a Surprise

I must work hard to block the memories of the cruel treatment I endured. Now, thinking about my first seven years in Africa makes me very happy no matter what I am doing. Because I get so sad when I think about that fateful morning on the wide river, I must not dwell too long on the subject. I will tell you as much as I can about my capture and voyage into slavery, but more time must pass before I can tell you everything. Attempting to recall more makes my hand shake, and then I cannot write. There is satisfaction from writing the few things that follow, and I avoid the panic caused by deeper recall.

When I got to Boston after three months of being chained in the dark, musty hold of a slave ship, I was weak and ailing. The slavers should have expected that their cargo would suffer. We were chained and packed shoulder to shoulder. We were not released to go to the bathroom, and so we had to lie in our own waste. I know I was healthy before my capture, so there is no doubt in my mind that the deplorable conditions on the slave ship caused my illness. I think this is one of those times in my life that a higher power took charge. I was too sick and confused to live without divine help.

Miss Chloe and the other servants in the Wheatley household fed and cared for me until I was able to work. I know that being chained in a filthy hold for three months must be the cause of my breathing problems. I did my best to hide my condition from the Wheatleys, because I did not want them to think me frail. Sick slaves are sold quickly before they die, and the master loses all of his money. If Mr. Wheatley thought I was in bad health, he would probably sell me, and I could become property of an abusive master. I do not think I could tolerate any more abuse.

In truth, Mrs. Wheatley's illness was foremost in Mr. Wheatley's mind, taking his attention away from my health. As long as I was in place ready to do his bidding each morning, I would not have to worry about being closely inspected for signs of being sick. After all, Mr. Wheatley bought me to care for his sick wife and not to be a spirited friend of family members. There was so much concern for Mrs. Wheatley that it kept anyone from noticing my tiredness.

I can remember the comfort I got by recalling the soft hum of my mother's morning prayers. As she explained it to me, those prayers were for the protection of our family. She would rise before the rest of us and place four polished black stones on the altar in our hut—one for each of us. Then she would pour water over each stone while chanting prayers to our god. She did not use the brown river water. She kept a jug of blue lake water that was used only for her morning prayer. It took many days and much effort to bring back water from the deep blue lake, so the jug was kept in a protected place. On the morning of my capture, I had left to go fishing before mother began her ritual. Because there were slavers in the area, I knew my parents would not allow me to go to the river by myself.

I remember thinking to myself in the quiet of my little room in the Wheatley house that the reason I was alive was that God had answered my mother's prayers. I know my parents are not Christian, but I am sure that my God is their God. My parents just have not been introduced to the real God yet. There is talk at our church of some day sending missionaries to Africa. I can only hope my true parents get a chance to hear what I have heard about God during my short time in this country.

I could not get the thought out of my mind that I would never see my family again. An image of my family stayed in my head even as I slept. I sometimes awoke and would briefly feel like I was home, only to realize I had been dreaming. It was difficult to eat, and what little food I managed to get down came right back up, sometimes tinged with blood. Miss Chloe warned me through our sign language and the few words that I understood that a sickly slave might be left to die, but I cared little for life. I felt so hopeless that I believed only death would cure my malaise.

"Your life's worth more than five shillings, girl," she said. I looked up at her and shrugged. Her words still meant little to me, but they had a lilting cadence that belied her brusque exterior. Later, when I learned English, I questioned Chloe about our early time together, and that is how I am able to piece together her words. Also, she still tells me that the Good Lord has a plan for me. How difficult it must have been for Chloe to prepare a little girl she considered her daughter for the life of a slave.

"I'm gonna keep feedin' you till you keep that food down. You may be nuthin' more than a pinch o' dirt to these white folks, but Jesus put you in my care, an' I ain't gonna let you die till He's ready to take you."

Chloe was a stubborn, determined woman, and her spark ignited a fire of hope within me. After a few weeks under her care, my health improved. As I grew stronger, I began to assume my share of the household duties. I watched and learned. During supper, two slaves would stand at the table and pass food to the Wheatleys; it was our job to anticipate what they wanted. If Nathaniel glanced at the gravy bowl, I would take it to him without his having to ask for gravy. There was never a comment made to us by the Wheatleys. To them we were not even there.

I did good work at the serving table, so it became one of my regular tasks. Although it wasn't a difficult chore, the Wheatleys ate before the slaves did, and this meant I always had to serve food with an empty stomach. Sometimes, I was so hungry that the smell of the food made my mouth water and my stomach gurgle. Chloe helped me again by telling me to swallow a spoonful of horse and mule feed before serving time. It actually tasted good, and it kept me from feeling hungry.

One day, many months after I had arrived, a new slave worked with me at table. He failed to notice Master Nathaniel's glance at the gravy bowl. Nathaniel waited a moment, but then grew impatient. In a harsh voice, he asked for the gravy. The slave did not know enough English to understand Nathaniel and did not react. Nathaniel glared at the gravy bowl and then pointed to it. At last, the new slave grasped what was wanted, and he picked up the bowl and brought it to young Master Nathaniel, spilling a few drops of gravy onto the linen tablecloth. I was aghast at what happened next.

Nathaniel ordered the slave to kneel. "Get on your knees, boy," he said. The slave stood mute, still not understanding his master's words. "Down," Nathaniel said. When the slave did not react, Nathaniel raised his voice. "Are you deaf as well as clumsy?"

Master Nathaniel's shouting did nothing to improve the slave's understanding, so Nathaniel stood up and kicked the poor man behind his knees, causing him to collapse. Even the other Wheatleys were shocked by what happened next. Nathaniel poured the hot gravy all over the slave. Later, on Nathaniel's orders, another slave gave the unfortunate man ten lashes with a whip.

Several months passed, and I learned many new things, including the art of sewing. I also learned to speak English with such speed that even my masters were impressed. One day, while dusting the furniture in the study, I chanced upon a leather-bound volume that lay open on a table. I leafed through it, not understanding the black markings on the pages, but they were drawn so finely and so uniformly that their beauty enthralled me. As I turned the pages, I failed to notice Mrs. Wheatley enter the room behind me.

"That's the Bible, child. Are you interested in it?"

Afraid that I had done something wrong, I slammed the book shut, curtsied to Mrs. Wheatley, and lowered my eyes to the floor, just as Miss Chloe had taught me.

"I didn't mean no harm, Ma'am," I said.

Mrs. Wheatley walked over to me and lifted my chin up so that she looked directly into my frightened eyes. "It's all right, child. It's a good thing to want to know God." She reached over to the book and opened it again. "These are God's words. If you would like, I'll teach them to you."

I risked a smile. Slaves were not allowed to look directly at white folks, but Mrs. Wheatley held my head and looked right into my eyes. I knew it would be wrong to close my eyes, so I did the only thing I could, and I did not feel like I was doing wrong. For a few moments, I felt loved. It was like looking into the eyes of your parent before sleep.

"Yes, Ma'am," I said. "I would like to learn." It was at that moment that my status in the household began to change. Mrs. Wheatley started teaching me to read and write. I don't know why she chose to do this, but after that, just about every day she gave me about an hour of instruction. When I began to read and write well, I often did the talking, and Mrs. Wheatley listened. We kept this hour to ourselves until Mrs. Wheatley got so sick she had to stop. Chloe was shocked by this turn of events; according to her, slaves were not supposed to read and write.

I began by learning the alphabet and was soon reading and writing simple words. Within a week, I was memorizing twenty-five new words a day. Mrs. Wheatley was so delighted by my progress that she rewarded me by spending more time reading stories from the Bible. These stories were at first mysterious to me, but, as each new chapter unfolded, my understanding increased.

The story of Noah reminded me of a tale the elders told at home. Just like Noah, Margay built an enormous boat. All the villagers laughed at him for his efforts; they laughed even harder when he filled his boat with animals —two of every kind. They were surprised to see lions walking tamely with goats, but even that improbable sight did not change their opinion of Margay's foolishness. They thought he was crazy. Then the rains came, and the villagers wondered, and when the rain didn't stop, and Margay and his family were safe in their boat with the animals, the villagers understood, but it was too late for them. They watched as Margay and his menagerie floated away, while everyone else remained behind to die in the flood. After many days had passed, the flood receded, and Margay, his family, and the animals left the boat. As the elders told us, the Fulani people are descendents of Margay.

Another book in the study that we often used was Dr. Samuel Johnson's dictionary. The dictionary contained thousands of words and their definitions, and it became one of my keys to unlocking the secrets of English reading and writing. I longed to have my own Bible and dictionary, but slaves were not allowed to own property, and certainly not books.

Although my health had improved, the Wheatleys became aware of my illness. I had a large lump on my neck that I could not hide. Then there were the coughing fits that the Wheatleys handled by sending me to my room for the entire day. I just knew that I would be sold while I was still presentable, but, instead of selling me, as Chloe said they might, they left me alone. I had become useful to them, and perhaps they thought that my health would improve eventually.

The Wheatleys began taking me with them everywhere they went, including to church. This was a strange new experience for me. At home, our religion was an integral part of nature, and we acknowledged the one God. In the Wheatleys' church, nature played no part in the worship, but the congregants believed in only one God. My father had taught me that our village could not survive with more than one chief and, therefore, he reasoned that the world could not survive with more than one God. So, using my father's thinking, I think I can accept any religion that believes there is only one God.

Although it was different from the spiritual singing I was accustomed to, the hymns the people chanted in church touched my soul. This was also true with the new language I was learning. English lacked the expressive, deep-throated sounds of Africa, but it possessed its own sweet melody; in the years to come, I grew to appreciate the images it painted in my head.

There were other aspects about the Wheatleys' church that disturbed me. Many of the parishioners kept slaves. I didn't understand how people who believed in God's love could own other human beings. The minister of the

Wheatleys' church, Reverend Samuel Cooper, did not own slaves, but I learned that some ministers of other churches did.

Chloe told me that Reverend Cooper's grandfather, Judge Samuel Sewall, wrote a book called *The Selling of Joseph* that used the words of the Bible to disprove the right to own slaves, but other people cited the Bible to prove that the opposite was true, and for many years, Judge Sewall and his family were ridiculed for their nonconformist beliefs.

One day, Mr. Wheatley gave the twins identical gold and leather Bibles. I was jealous. Mary and Nathaniel had the freedom to read anytime they wanted, but they seldom did so. If Mr. Wheatley had given me a Bible, I would have spent every free moment reading it.

Although he didn't give me a Bible, Mr. Wheatley did give me a calendar for the year 1762. From it, I learned numbers. He also gave me a quill pen, which he demonstrated by circling the number 15 in the month of April.

"That's the day you became a member of the Wheatley household, child," he said.

He was trying to be kind; another master would have said, "That's the day I bought you." I dared to hope that he viewed me as something more than property.

Mrs. Wheatley, noting how much I used the calendar, gave me a new one the following year along with a pen, a bundle of quills, and some leftover ink. I was thus able to record my own words.

The requirements of my servitude in the Wheatley household limited any pleasure I found in reading and writing. What little time I had to myself was mostly devoted to rest, but I forced myself to read and write by the light of a tallow candle at least an hour each night before I slept. I would sneak a volume from the library at night and, each morning, I would awake with a book clutched close to my breast like a feeding infant. I was careful with the Wheatleys' books, but the possibility of damaging their property didn't stop me. I reasoned that the Wheatleys wouldn't notice a crumpled page or two because I never saw anyone else read those books; they seemed to care only that I dust them once a week.

To me, books were like magic that only white people controlled. In Africa, we had no books—only storytellers and history keepers who had a special gift for remembering. They were like talking books. They made sure everyone knew what was happening, and they kept us entertained. In America, a white person can buy a book and read it anytime. For me, this is magic.

Once something is written, it cannot be changed, but, when told aloud, it can be altered at a whim. Teaching stories stayed the same, but fun stories changed to fit the audience. Our history keepers took an oath to tell the truth. The history keeper was also responsible for giving what I can best describe as an oral broadsheet.

One Sunday, without any explanation, Mrs. Wheatley handed me a box. I was so engrossed in reading the tag attached to it that I failed to notice that the whole family was watching me. I said each letter aloud, mentally associating the letter with the proper sound. I felt embarrassed by my awkwardness in deciphering my own name.

I must have been the most confused little girl in Boston. The notion of giving was as important to my people in Africa as it was to the white people in America, but Americans saw me as a savage. Why would they make a gift to a savage?

What if this wasn't a gift? What if it was a trick? I wasn't sure. Suddenly, I became afraid as I thought about the consequences of having mishandled my owners' books. I had seen slaves chained and beaten for misuse of their master's property.

Mrs. Wheatley said, "Louisa, open your gift."

I pointed to the gift and then to myself. I said, "For me? Is it really for me?"

As one, the Wheatleys said, "Open your present, Louisa."

I opened the box. As soon as I saw what was inside, I said, "Huuuu!" This African cry was all my lips could form. The English words to express thanks escaped my mind. At last, I looked up and saw the pleased expressions on the Wheatleys' faces, and I said, "I have my own Bible. My own Bible!"

They had given me a Bible! I owned not just a book, but *The* Book! I felt obliged not only to read it, but also to mold my life around its contents.

That Bible changed my life, but it also increased my confusion about my relationship with the Wheatleys. They had treated me with respect and with affection, but I remained their property. If one must be a slave, then there could be no better masters than the Wheatleys; but the fact of enforced servitude permeated every aspect of my life—even the pleasure of receiving a gift.

I was only nine years old. My life should have been spent playing and being loved by my family. Instead, I was a slave. I tried to imagine changing places with little Nat or Mary Wheatley, and what their lives might have been like had they been owned by my parents. I think my father and mother would have loved them, and I dared to hope that the Wheatley family was beginning to love me. It was difficult to imagine Nat and Mary as slaves; it was even more difficult accepting the fact that I was a slave, and that I would never enjoy a real childhood.

Such thoughts frustrated me and made me miserable, and they were dangerous. Masters wanted their slaves to remember nothing of Africa. They gave us new names, and they forbade us to speak our native tongue, but I remembered.

Sometimes, when I was at the market, I saw other people from my tribe. Like me, they had left the safety of the village to fish or hunt and were captured by slavers. At such times, we spoke our own language and recalled the old days when we were free and surrounded by family and friends. They assured me that my father had moved the village so far into the jungle that they would be safe from the slavers. There was mention that my brother had been on one of the hunting trips and could have been captured. We always talked secretly, out of earshot of white folks.

But how is memory dreaded by the race,
Who scorn her warnings, and defile her grace?
By he unveil'd each horrid crime appears,
Her awful hand a cup of wormwood bears.
Days, years misspent, O what a hell of woe!
Hers the worst tortures that our souls can know.

Phillis Wheatley

Chapter 4—Fifteen Years of Learning While Performing Slave Labor

It was my good luck to meet Obour Tanner. There was no way a little, ten-year-old African slave girl, who worked from sunup to sundown, would likely meet another young African girl, much less one so similar to herself. I know the Lord placed Obour in my life at precisely the time I most needed a friend.

Obour did not stare at the ground like many slaves, but stood statuesque, with a simple smile brightening her face. Her diction was crisp and the sentence structure correct, even though, like me, she had been in this country only about a year. She wore old, discarded clothing, but it was not spotted or tattered. Most slaves were tired at the end of the day and would not take the time to patch and clean their clothes. Acceptance of a ragged appearance meant they could get a few more minutes of sleep. Obour and I both took the time to repair and clean our clothes because our pride simply would not allow otherwise.

As I think back, I realize how much I enjoyed Obour's friendship. Our closeness and the freedom given me while visiting the Craigs made me look forward to the Rhode Island trips with intense expectation. I still get excited just thinking about my trips to the Craigs. I can also tell you that after seventeen years in America, I no longer yearn for home. I have accepted my fate as a former slave and now a free American.

Perhaps my first trip to Rhode Island stands out more than the others. The hot, humid July day was so similar to African weather that it intensified my desire to be home. Then my eyes were drawn to African colors. When I got closer and saw Obour's African quilt hanging over her fence, my knees gave way, sending me headfirst onto the boardwalk leading up to the Craigs' mansion. Now I know it sounds strange that I would pass out just from seeing a quilt, but you must understand my life had been devoid of color and artistry until I laid eyes on Obour's quilt. For almost a year, it was as if all I saw were shades of gray and white, and then, lit by a bright summer sun, just a few feet away was a magnificent African quilt full of the rich colors of my birthplace. For a moment, I was back on the African plain, and a powerful joy caused me to call my father's name. Just as quickly, I returned to reality, but with a racing heart and weakened legs. No longer able to keep my balance, I collapsed.

Lying on the ground, too weak to immediately get to my feet, I caught sight of Obour peeping out the front door of her little cabin. I looked at the eyes staring at me and wondered if a slave could possibly have something as nice as private quarters. I found out that with a benevolent master like Dr. Craig, even a slave could have a private residence.

Beginning with that first visit to Rhode Island, and each year thereafter, Mr. Wheatley relaxed his control and gave me the same amount of free time that Dr. Craig gave Obour. Free time for a few fortunate house servants became a Wheatley tradition during family vacation. I must admit to being jealous of Obour, knowing she had that freedom every day.

Obour told me that Dr. Craig often gave her liberty on Sunday after the noon meal, and she returned to slave status only at the beginning of supper or when the large bell was rung three times. My taste of freedom came only once a year when we visited the Craigs, but that taste was all it took to make me crave freedom with every nerve in my body. Mrs. Wheatley told me that she would give me my freedom on her death. When the Good Lord took my Mistress, I feared my Master would not follow his wife's directions, but Mr. Wheatley remained true to his word and freed me. When he said the words, "Louisa, you are now free," an emotional dam burst, and I could do nothing but cry uncontrollably. Even now I am unable to put into words my feelings. Thankful, grateful—no word adequately describes being released from slavery.

The Wheatleys vacationed in Newport, Rhode Island, from the middle of July until August every year. In 1775, they moved to Rhode Island because their front yard had become a battleground in the fight to rid Boston of British troops. I think they also wanted to be close to their daughter and her husband, who lived in Providence. The pleasant vacation place in Newport became a shelter to protect us from attacks by the Redcoats.

My mistress died the year preceding the war with Great Britain. She set me free on her deathbed, and Mr. Wheatley complied with her wishes. I continued to serve Mr. Wheatley, but had the freedom to leave at any time. I used that freedom to return to Boston for an honor that few people, especially a black female former slave, have ever received—but I am getting ahead of myself.

It was fate that caused me to meet Obour Tanner and to enjoy the influence of the kind Doctor Craig on my master. Because the Craig family treated Obour as a human being, my owners treated me similarly. Had the Wheatleys not known the Craigs I am sure my life would have been much more difficult. In my heart, I knew the powerful love of my African mother and father kept me alive in a foreign place full of hate and meanness. Meeting a fellow African with that same love inside her refreshed my soul and gave me the strength of an African Princess. On my first visit to the Craigs, Obour and I spent every minute of our time together talking about Africa. As the years passed I relished each summer because Obour and I kept alive our African heritage.

Obour enjoyed learning just as I did. Much of my education was accidental as a result of serving the twins during their tutoring sessions. I did have the daily hour with Mrs. Wheatley, but she was not as educated as Dr. Craig, and I was given access to books, but only after I had done all of my chores. Dr. Craig allowed Obour to use his books, and he taught her how to help him in his practice of medicine.

During our two-week stay in Newport, my mistress released me from constant vigilance. A good house servant anticipated needs or was always within a whisper of being told what to do. This required hours of my time being spent just standing like a statue with a polite smile on my face. I used this time to create poetry in my head or to recall my brief seven years of freedom in Africa. While in Rhode Island, Obour and I were allowed to get away from our people and spend time together.

Obour lived in a small two-room cottage outside the main house. This was much nicer than my single room in the attic of the Wheatleys' house. The best thing about Obour's place was her small flower garden in front and her vegetable garden in back. She had time to take care of the gardens because Dr. Craig released her after the last meal. I had to work until my mistress was asleep and the master dismissed me. I said the best thing about Obour's place was her gardens, but I should have said her library. Books lined the walls of Obour's cottage, enclosing its occupant in a shell of knowledge.

Whenever the Craigs bought a new female slave, they asked Obour to care for her until the slave was able to function on her own. This did not happen often, because Dr. Craig was trying to wean himself from the use of slaves. He sometimes bought slaves to protect them from abusive owners.

Obour had a secret vault under her floor—a large metal box buried directly under five boards in the middle of her first room—in which she stored the most beautiful African beads and scarves. The kindly Dr. Craig, knowing how much pleasure Obour received from getting beads, buttons, combs, and scarves, often presented her with these items at the end of grueling work days.

It was not until the third summer that Obour showed me this secret hiding place. On the second day of the Wheatley vacation, without a word of warning, Obour left me sitting while she fetched an iron bar by the back door. She placed the bar in a knothole and pried up a floor board. I saw that there was only one nail going all the way through the board. The others were all cut off flush with the bottom of the board. Once that board was pried up, Obour pulled up four more boards with her hands. I could see the ground under the cabin and what looked like an old piece of scrap leather held in place by some foundation stones.

Obour rolled the stones aside, picked up the leather piece and folded it into a small square. She heard a noise and quickly checked for visitors—it was only the Craigs' hound paying us a visit. Obour then used an old spade to remove about a foot of dirt, and I saw the top of a metal box. She pulled the box inside the cabin, and with the most serene look on her face, opened it up to reveal an array of colorful items that could turn a slave dress into a royal gown. We would then spend our free time adorning ourselves with Obour's treasures and reliving the precious few years we had with Mother Africa. Before the masters called us to help at supper, it was always painful, but necessary, to replace the metal box until the next summer.

I love my friend Obour and feel no jealousy because she has a better life. As good as she has it, she is a slave like me. Having been a slave limits any good fortune we have on this earth. How can you enjoy anything if you have no hope for freedom? However, they could not control my thoughts, and my powerful thoughts give me a freedom that I know few people are privileged to have. I thank the Lord every day for His gift.

The Bible tells us to be content with the things we have, and I am truly contented. My contentment lies within me. On the outside, I am poor and sick, but on the inside, I am rich and vibrant. I think the Bible must be talking about inner contentment when it speaks of being content with all things. It also says that if you have everything you want, but lack inner contentment, then you are miserable.

I remember the first trip to Newport when I spotted Obour's quilt hanging on her fence. The colors and design immediately brought to mind the Senegal Katag. The closest English word to describe Katag would be wrestling matches. I must give you some glimpses of Africa in order for you to understand this African woman who, to this day, dearly misses her motherland.

Every year during the dry season, teams of adolescents came to my village from the surrounding countryside to take part in the Katag. The families of team members would march into the village first, dressed in what Americans would consider obscene costumes. The Atlantic coast of Africa is relatively humid, and so we wear clothing comfortable for such a climate. Each village had certain primary colors that could be seen in every item that came from the village. My village colors were dark blue, made from the berries of a tall, big-leafed plant; orange, made from tree bark; and sun bleached white.

I recognized the brown, yellow, and green design on Obour's quilt as the village colors of the final Katag match that took place just a few months before I was captured. The matches always coincided with the transition period between the dry and wet season. On the underside of my father's thatch-roofed headquarters hung the colors and designs of the neighboring tribes. I took many a nap in that huge headquarters building gazing at that beautiful display until the Wingush sealed my eyes. Storytellers told us about a tiny, fairy-like creature called the Wingush. The Wingush flew to every bed and brought special sand to paint on our eyelids to help us sleep soundly.

The very first day I arrived in Newport, Obour and I were able to sit down together on her front porch and talk. The kind Dr. Craig said something to the effect of "Let's dismiss the servants and have a private visit for a few hours before supper." Mr. Wheatley could only accept his friend's proposal, because to have said "no" would have been embarrassing. Dr. Craig told Obour he would ring the dinner bell when it was time for us to help prepare the evening meal.

I could not believe I was going to be able to talk with an African who came from near my village. If Dr. Craig had been the usual master, I would not have been able to talk with Obour until we had retired for the night. House slaves had to act like human statues. We wanted to be asked to do something, because just standing around for hours was perhaps our most difficult job.

Because our villages were so close together in Africa, we shared a common tongue. We both remembered the last Katag. I was only six at the time, and Obour was nine. We laughed when, at the same time, both of us mentioned the handsome young men. They wore leg bands made from Palmyra fibers, and the men from Obour's tribe wore belts with long fiber fringes. Our young men had short fibers and copper wrist bands. Neither tribe had elaborate headdresses, except for three sea eagle feathers stuck in their hair.

Obour helped me recall the singing, the dancing, and the parade that snaked through the village and then encircled a field large enough for ten matches to go on at the same time. Before the matches began, there was a special ceremony honoring last year's champion, who is no longer able to compete in the games. My brother was the honored champion of the last Katag I attended. Obour remembered him because he danced on her scarf at the conclusion of the ceremony. It is a very great honor for the champion to dance on a scarf dropped in front of him.

Sadly, Obour told me that my brother was captured by slavers not long after me. She herself was captured the following year. Having villages so close to the river made it too easy for the heavily armed slavers to snatch our people at whim. Who could have ever dreamed of buying and selling human beings when the decision was made to build our village close to the river?

Obour and I laughed at what the colonists called celebration music, mostly made with squeaky fiddles. In Africa, big drums sent a throbbing beat you could feel in the soles of your feet as well as in your soul.

Like the drums, you could feel the music coming from my favorite African stringed instrument—the ekontin, which is made from calabash gourds with long bamboo necks and three strings. The ekontin players would stand on high ground so the music rushed over us in a shower of notes. Obour and I decided to make an ekontin providing she could find some calabash seed for her garden. Things were relatively calm in Rhode Island and Boston, so we supposed that sometime within the next few summers we would be able to have an African celebration complete with the native instruments we intended to make. Just the thought, and numerous discussions about our proposed celebration, made the summers joyous occasions for both of us.

However, even the good Dr. Craig would not allow us to gather other servants for a celebration. There was some concern also about the instruments we were making being some sort of devices that could be used to incite slaves. Eventually, we had to give up the idea of an African celebration in America and simply continue to share our memories.

For roughly the next ten years, it seemed that peace surrounded our region. The French, Spanish, and English held claim to portions of America, and fights would occur between these nations as they tried to amass more land. These battles were fought in the wilds, not in Boston or Rhode Island.

Another privilege given me was keeping the broadsheets in my room after all of the family members had read them. Only Mr. Wheatley actually spent any time with the paper; the rest of the family preferred not to read the news. From those papers, I knew there was trouble in distant places like Detroit and Florida. It is worth noting that the name Colonel Washington often appeared in stories about colonists helping the British protect their land holdings.

During this calm ten years, I began to write poetry in earnest. My mistress relished any opportunity to visit other wealthy Bostonians, and those opportunities were many, as long as she brought her slave to recite poetry. I brag too much. Mrs. Wheatley needed me to help her walk as her illness made her very weak. She so loved to socialize that I often dressed her in her sick bed and bore her weight as we she leaned on me for support. No one had the heart to ask her to stay home.

Around 1773, I began to hear complaints from my master and his friends about new taxes imposed on us by England. The tax problem touched me directly when broadsheet prices doubled. Limits had to be set, and printing news was more important than a weekly helping of poetry. I not only lost my income, but also the pleasure of sharing my poetry with others. The British would allow the colonies to buy only specially marked paper for printing newspapers and all of the other documents that were now a major part of life in the colonies.

According to the English Parliament, the colonies had to bear some of the costs of keeping so many British soldiers over here. Mr. Wheatley profited from sales to British troops, but worked very hard to get the tax repealed. According to Mr. Wheatley, it was wrong to pay taxes if we did not have someone representing us in Parliament.

I've already told you about visiting Newport, but every so often, Dr. Craig would bring his family to Boston. On those occasions, through the influence of Dr. Craig, I was dismissed for a morning or afternoon to simply enjoy the company of my friend Obour. One afternoon, we found ourselves walking along the harbor, and for the first time we saw an African manning one of the many little booths at the market. He was selling paintings of vistas from the motherland. I felt at one with him because I was also an artist of sorts. I created with words and he with paint. I had no money, so I could enjoy his work only for that moment, but when I got home, I knew I would make permanent the joy of that moment in poetry.

Our walk also exposed us to a ship unloading slaves. We saw two little girls who reminded us of ourselves when we arrived in this country just a few years ago. There was only one response available to us, and that was no response. We could say or do nothing to help those poor little girls. We both became weak and had to sit down on a wall. We tried not to draw attention to ourselves but could not hold back tears of anguish. Would this country follow England's lead and rid itself of this world's most despicable trade—selling human beings? We composed ourselves and continued our walk as we both prayed for the abolition of slavery.

That night after supper, I had the delightful experience of creating a poem with the immediate approval of my friend. The Craigs spent the night, and so Obour and I were allowed to spend together the period between finishing all the chores and bedtime. Obour helped me with the chores, so there would be more time than usual. Obour enjoyed reading the poem I wrote about the African artist we had seen that morning. She was amazed at how fast I produced the lines and how I caught with words the event just as we experienced it. She asked permission to make a copy, and I gladly gave it.

Near the end of this peaceful ten years, I wrote my first major work, an elegy for Minister George Whitefield. As I wrote it, I thought about the two little girls Obour and I saw being unloaded in Boston Harbor. I thought about how strongly Reverend Whitefield hated slavery. He risked his life when he spoke in large halls before hundreds of people. Whitefield's oratory inflamed the hearts of abolitionists and quieted the tongues of slavers.

You should also know that near the end of my peaceful ten years, the colonies were beginning organized resistance to the British Government. Representatives from nine colonies met in New York and drew up a declaration of rights and liberties. In Boston, there was a strong protest movement against over-taxation. Especially repugnant to Bostonians was the tax the British levied on tea. It seemed as if my ten years of peace might end at the same time that the peace in the colonies seemed to be waning.

A Hymn to Humanity

Can Afric's muse forgetful prove?
Or can such friendship fail to move
A tender human heart?

Phillis Wheatley

Chapter 5—A Blessed Slave

Ages Seven to Twelve

On April 15, just a year after I arrived in Boston, the Wheatleys gave me a Bible. Then on July 15 they took me with them on their vacation to Rhode Island. They made it very clear that the Bible was not a birthday gift, but rather a gift I happened to receive on my designated birthday. They also made it plain that the liberties I enjoyed on vacation were just temporary and due to their friendship with the Craigs. Every year, as April 15 got closer, I started thinking about the day I got the gift. As July 15 drew near, I began to think about my friend Obour and those wonderful hours of freedom.

My mistress told me that, for years, she believed that gift-giving was sinful, but she and the rest of the family were changing. They started to break away from those strict beliefs when they gave me a Bible. Their concerned looks showed how uneasy they felt not following the old ways, but you could also tell that they enjoyed the new opportunities a less strict belief gave them. I tried to make them feel better by telling them over and over again how much I appreciated getting my own copy of the Bible. I reminded the Wheatleys of their other gifts to me during the year. Having such a grateful slave and reminding them that they gave me gifts on other occasions put the Wheatleys at ease and allowed us to enjoy the moment.

I thought about how similar my baptism was to an African celebration. In Africa, we usually celebrated outside in the fresh air where we could jump and sway to the music that pounded in rhythm with our hearts. The elders, unable to dance vigorously, sat as a group and encouraged the young people with their radiant smiles and rhythmic clapping. For my baptism in America, the festivity moved outside, and the people showed their happiness with music and shouts of joy. I wondered why we did not have church outside more often, especially since it put everyone in such a wonderful mood. I was perplexed to be among people who needed God confined to a building. Colonists seemed to be in a constant state of unhappiness.

I knew I was being used as a trial for the Methodist practices of slave baptism and giving birthday presents. Shortly after the Wheatleys bought me, they began the process of changing from Puritans to Methodists. I rather enjoyed being part of their change process, because it added some zest to the otherwise dull life of a house servant. Looking back, I can appreciate the courage of the Wheatleys as they broke from the firmly foreboding Puritanism.

Knowing that the rigid Wheatleys were open to change moved me to think about my own life. After going to church with them for nearly a year, I decided I wanted to become a Christian. I told Mistress Wheatley my desire, and she said she would ask the minister if he would baptize me. Just a few months later, I found myself being called to the pulpit and asked if I accepted Christ as my Savior. My answer was a simple yes. That is all it took. Well, there was a little more. I had to stand before the entire congregation and give my testimony.

My mistress prepared me well, and I felt tremendous relief as I told the church how Christ loved me. A shy slave girl stood before a crowd of white people and told her conversion story without faltering. As I finished my statement, tears flowed down my cheeks. Looking out, I could not help but notice most members were also in tears. The minister hugged me and announced that I would receive baptism next Sunday. There I stood, a slave whose soul was about to be washed and set free, while the frail body would continue to labor—but now for the glory of God.

The next Sunday was a beautiful spring day. Mrs. Wheatley gave me the most gorgeous white dress complete with a veil. I was the only person baptized that day, so I could not help but feel important for the first time since stepping onto American soil. I also felt deeply loved.

The entire congregation walked in song past the Revere house to the baptismal pool on River Witham. The minister had me affirm to the people encircling the pool that I wanted baptism and communion with the church. I replied that I loved the Lord and would be honored to be His servant. At that, the minister took my hand and led me to the very edge of the pool. I stepped out of my new shoes and felt the cold mud on my bare feet. The minister then walked out into the water in his Sunday clothes. I followed, unaware that I was even wearing the beautiful white dress. We walked hand in hand until we were waist deep.

The minister's piercing blue eyes held my attention as he put one arm on my back and the other lightly on my chest. He said in a loud booming voice, "Sister Louisa Wheatley, I baptize you in the name of the Father, Son, and Holy Ghost." Simultaneously, he guided me down into the water where I stayed submerged for a fair amount of time. I came up gasping for air and overjoyed. The people sang as the minister and I walked together out of the Witham pool. At last, I was a Christian.

I carried my shoes as we walked back to the church. I was concerned about my clothing, but there was so much happiness in the group that concern soon left. At the church, my Mistress led me into a beautiful room where she helped me clean up and change. The day concluded with a special meal, at which I was the guest of honor and got to sit with the white people.

When she prepared me for baptism, Mrs. Wheatley saw my gift for learning. She often got interested in my answers and asked me how I could give such complete, detailed responses with so little education. I told her I listened very closely at every Sunday and Wednesday night church service and reminded her that I owned my own Bible. I read every chance I got. After one year in America, I could read and write English as well as Mary and Nathaniel.

Mrs. Wheatley kept me by her side because of need and a powerful attachment similar to a mother-daughter relationship. However, both Mrs. Wheatley and I knew the strong bonds of slavery would never allow her to display her motherly instincts. She took great comfort in the knowledge that I epitomized the obedient servant.

She did not know my obedience resulted from the brief time I spent with my real parents and not from the cruel array of fears imposed on slaves by their owners. Talk flowed around me as if I were a pet, instead of a little girl. Because I was African property, not a family member, people regularly spoke their uncensored thoughts in my presence.

Mr. Wheatley tended toward loyalty to the crown and often had British houseguests. He sometimes talked with his friends about declaring independence. Mr. Wheatley would pay a heavy price if we separated from England. Most of his business and wealth depended on British relationships. Our best and most popular fabrics came from mills in England, and we also supplied several London stores with our finished goods. A war with Great Britain would effectively close down the Wheatley enterprises.

I appreciated British abolitionists because, for humanitarian reasons, they wanted to end slavery. Naturally, I kept these thoughts to myself. I was also aware of English hypocrisy, whereby they spoke against slavery while maintaining the lucrative "middle passage" slave trade.

When the ship docked in the West Indies, the slaves became fodder for the men's pleasure. With no sailing duties to occupy their minds, they quickly turned on their shackled cargo. While the others took shore leave, the sailors left on board to stand guard abused them unmercifully, out of anger at having to stay behind while their friends enjoyed themselves on the island.

The returning sailors were even worse than the angry guards, because their actions were bolstered by too much rum. A little seven-year-old girl became prey for drunken sailors. Because of this abuse, I felt some disgust for things British. I knew the London market provided great wealth for the Wheatleys. A friend told me that it takes money to beget money, so I should look past the source to the sizable sum the Wheatleys could amass. Following that advice, I listened passively to the talk praising Britain, and concentrated on my servant duties.

A war would ruin all the plans and preparations for Nathaniel's active participation in the Wheatley Corporation.

As early as 1766, one could feel the tension between supporters of British control and those who talked about the colonies gaining self-rule. Over the next ten years, I watched as the push for independence became stronger and stronger. Finally, in 1775, the Wheatleys moved out of Boston to Rhode Island in anticipation of a war with Great Britain. With so many British troops in Boston, Mr. Wheatley knew their home could be in the middle of a battlefield. By that time, I had been granted my freedom. Mary Wheatley was very worried about me and invited me to stay with her and her husband in Providence, Rhode Island. It was while I was in Providence that I wrote about the godlike George Washington.

It was strange to me that Americans were willing to make war over the detested unfair British taxation practices, but thought nothing about the cruel practice of slavery. With few exceptions, only muted protests were uttered against enslavement of Africans, but there was a huge uproar over the cost of tea. A revolution would be costly, but our country will recuperate within a few years whether we win or lose. However, it will take centuries to recover from slavery, and that recovery will only begin when we get our freedom.

Mrs. Wheatley was very active in her church. As her personal servant, I attended most church events with her, which, as I've said, led to my conversion to the Christian faith. My gift for writing and reading earned me the special privilege of taking part in church services.

I knew that convenience rather than love dictated my being able to participate in church activities. However, as time passed I could sense some people wanted to relate to me in a more humane way. The services I provided, tributes, poems, and animated readings, could not be done as well by anyone else. Still, they treated me like a trained animal and thanked my keeper, Mistress Wheatley, rather than showing any appreciation to me for my talents. Some members quietly thanked me, but spoke so low I could barely hear them. At least, they tried to be polite, but their efforts to conceal praising a slave left me with an even greater feeling of disgust.

At first, I was embarrassed by being the only African allowed to take part in white church services. How did the other slaves confined to the "slave gallery" of church feel when I made my appearances at the altar? My question was answered one day when a slave asked to speak with me. We were both waiting for our masters outside the barbershop.

The old slave was bent and gnarled much like the weathered trees that grew on top of Bunker Hill. His arms did not make normal angles and were so contorted they appeared useless, but someway, the old slave managed to use one useless arm to tip his hat as he approached me, making that act of respect even more meaningful.

Mrs. Wheatley did not want me to socialize with other slaves. I did not agree with her request, but my extreme shyness made talking with strangers difficult. Still, I felt a strong bond with other black people, and I hated being told not to talk with other Africans.

I decided to talk with the old slave and told him how much I appreciated his kindness. How could I refuse to talk with such a polite person who was much older than I? What followed was a surprise. I was not prepared for his stumbling speech or the praise he heaped on me.

The man spoke crude English. He must have been practicing his very proper and polite request to speak to me for months. The expression on his face said much more than his crumbled words. With an angelic smile that tore at my heart, he said:

"Me so proud of you. You special. You our American Queen. Thank you."

As his master came out of the barbershop, the old slave ended by saying, "Please make us proud more."

After that beautiful thought flowed from his mouth, he politely bowed and ran to his master. I had no time for a reply.

This was my day for being praised. No sooner had he left, when another slave asked me if I was the same Louisa Wheatley who wrote poems for the broadsheet and elegies for white people. I told him that I was indeed Louisa Wheatley, and yes, I wrote elegies and poetry. Using much better diction, this slave told me how proud he was when he saw a black person delivering an elegy or when he read one of my poems in the local newspaper. Then someone across the street signaled this gentleman, and he also had to take his leave before I could say a word.

These chance meetings with slaves who held me in such high esteem set up the goal within me to strive to those lofty expectations. I had mistakenly thought fellow slaves would be jealous. The reality was that my successes gave them the rare delight of knowing a slave could perform as well if not better than white people. The attention and praise from fellow slaves made me want to do everything I could to help my people. We did not ask to come to this country, but now it is our new home.

Very little money came to me from the publication of my work. Mr. Wheatley kept most of it. Mrs. Wheatley put a small portion of what I made in an account set aside for me for when I became free. I published so many things that the small amounts added up to a sizable sum. I was concerned that the Wheatleys would take this money and use it themselves. To their credit, my fears were unfounded.

My writing soon made me well-known all around the Boston area. I was surprised to read a story about myself in the local newspaper. In Africa, this would have been kept in the memory of a teller, who would then give the information to the large groups that formed around him several times during the day and night. I cannot remember ever being the subject of a teller's story, but it sure felt good to read about myself in the newspaper.

To become a village teller was an honor given to people with special gifts. I act like a teller when I record important events in my poems and prose. I feel especially good when thousands of people get to read my work after it is in print. If Boston had tellers, and I was not a slave, I would love to have the job.

I also realized, with the exception of my capture, how sheltered a life I lived. Until age seven, I was the pampered daughter of an African chief. On arrival in Boston, the Wheatleys bought me and soon realized I could earn them a handsome profit. To protect their new source of income, they gave me special treatment. I realized that most slaves were not allowed to learn out of fear of an uprising if slaves were allowed an education. Being kept uneducated was a far greater restraint than our shackles.

Some families treated their slaves more like free people than slaves. After about five years, the Wheatleys began treating me with respect normally reserved for free whites. It was difficult to accept because it seemed to me that other slaves drew the harsh treatment from which I was excused. My instincts kept me wary, and I knew of many slaves who suffered, some even death, when they thought their owners cared about them.

A few saintly people in Boston risked losing their lives when they spoke out in public about the need to stop slavery. More common were people who talked about ending slavery, but did nothing to end the immoral practice.

Some ministers preached about slaves being children of God and for the need to end slavery. I was especially pleased when the Rev. Jonathan Sewall agreed with me that Christian slaveholders were hypocrites. I later used the phrase "Christian hypocrites" in a letter to Rev. Sampson Occom who, interestingly, was a Mohegan Indian. Indians got the same harsh treatment that slaves got in Boston. Samuel Sewall, a high court justice and the father of Jonathan, set a fine example for his son when he wrote a powerful anti-slavery tract that caused quite a disturbance in Boston.

Benjamin Franklin, a well-known colonist, wanted to free slaves and end slavery. He visited with me while I was in London, and we discussed our mutual friend, British abolitionist, Rev. George Whitefield. I owe my acceptance of Christ to the sermons of the Rev. Whitefield.

I often think about my decision to become a Christian. My heart made the decision to join the church in spite of the bigotry displayed by most members and some ministers. Going to church where some people thought I was less than human was difficult, but for every mean person in the church, there were three people who were kind and helpful. People were even nicer to me after the minister thanked me from the pulpit for my poems and elegies.

Around the age of nine, I realized that my talents got me preferential treatment in the Wheatley manor. When I traveled outside the neighborhood, I had to submit to the harsh, unfair treatment imposed on all slaves. However, being from the Wheatley home gave me some protection from malcontents.

Eventually, the Wheatleys allowed me to use their library, which I later learned was unusual even for kindly slave owners. I no longer had to sneak books from the library. I think the Wheatleys knew I was using books and decided not to punish me, but to allow me to read. They seemed unconcerned about breaking with the custom of denying slaves access to books. Bostonians thought it would be unnatural for a slave to read. They thought that nature kept slaves from reading, and so laws doing the same thing were unnecessary. Had there been a slave literacy law in Boston, the Wheatleys—who were law-abiding—would never have broken it.

Southern colonies made harsh slave literacy laws, because they were dependent on slave labor to plant and harvest their crops. They knew smart slaves would not tolerate the terrible working conditions and mistreatment so common in the South. In the North, most households kept only a few slaves. For example, the Wheatleys kept between twelve and fifteen. Some Southern plantations kept hundreds of slaves, and even a small farm would have at least fifty Africans. It was because slaves so greatly out-numbered the free people that Southerners feared a slave rebellion.

I think the Wheatleys got pleasure knowing someone was using the books they received as gifts from their British friends. I could spend many delightful hours telling Mrs. Wheatley what I had been reading. She, in turn, talked with her friends as if she had read the books. By parroting my summaries, Mrs. Wheatley became one of the most popular members of her social group.

One day, Mrs. Wheatley said to me,
"Please tell me as much as you can about Milton, so I won't feel so left out when the ladies talk about him."

I told Mrs. Wheatley that Milton began writing poetry at the age of ten. She stopped me before I could complete another sentence, and said,

"Louisa, you wrote that beautiful elegy just a few weeks ago, and you are only ten."

I told her that Milton was such a powerful writer he influenced everything I did. I recommended *Paradise Lost* to her, a book I was struggling to understand, and told her that reading Milton helped me understand how to write about good and evil.

Mrs. Wheatley wanted to hear about how Milton studied the heavens with his telescope. I could not tell her that I also studied the stars. It would be unlikely, but possible for her to find out, that I hid night navigation tips in my writing. I put directions for safe travel to five free areas I called "landscapes in realms above" in my poem about an African painter. I used phrases for the North Star, like "heavenly transport glow," that slaves understood.

I told my Mistress about Milton enduring blindness, and she gasped as I said that I had to put up with slavery. Mrs. Wheatley was so interested in Milton, she bade me read *Paradise Lost* aloud to her. I was happy to fulfill her request and felt I did an especially good job reading about the fall of mankind.

Embedded in my mind is how my mistress overlooked my slave status when she needed my intellect. She sometimes talked to me as if I was a friend or family member. I so wanted to be loved that, even after years of this treatment, she could get whatever she wanted from me with her cruel deceptions. Then, when she got what she wanted, the friendly manner stopped, and I would be ordered to carry out a menial task. Somehow, the Wheatley family thought that owning only 15 Africans kept them from the vile ranks of slave holders.

April 15, 1765, marked what I thought was my twelfth birthday, although I could not be sure. With great fondness, I recalled my first birthday about a year after the Wheatleys bought me. That year, I managed to give both Mr. and Mrs. Wheatley a gift. I wanted to present the gifts on their birthdays, but neither would divulge the dates. They also warned me that Puritans did not celebrate birthdays.

The people from my country know how to enjoy life. Americans are gloomy and think it is wrong to have fun. I especially liked Africa in the fall. All the people feasted on the finest products of the new harvest. After eating, storytellers used words and costumed actors to create another place right before our eyes. I can still recall the elaborate costumes created in absolute secrecy for the big fall event. Not even my father, the chief, was allowed to preview the fall play. We had a similar celebration for each season of the year. There are also big events for births, deaths, star changes, and memorable storms. The greatest celebrations took place when a villager passed into eternity. A minimum of three days were set apart for these occasions. On the first day, we recalled the person's life with many testimonials. The next day was spent preparing the body for its final day on earth. It is rubbed with pungent oils and covered with sweet-smelling herbs. Finally, it is wrapped in a long, white garment and placed on a funeral pyre. On the last day of the funeral, the pyre is lit as the entire village chants songs to the Great Spirit. The villager's ashes, mingled with wood and earth, are put in a boat made from woven palms and launched in the Senegal River. If I ever have the chance, I want to teach America to celebrate like Mother Africa.

I could not spend what little money I had, so I wrote poems for Wheatley family members on the back of fancy advertising paper. I got the paper from Mr. Wheatley's trash. I made frames from tree limbs, and Mr. Revere, our silversmith, gave me some glass. The Wheatleys hung my gifts in the main room. I bubbled over inside with good feelings whenever Mrs. Wheatley pointed them out to guests. However, Mrs. Wheatley never told anyone that the gifts were from me. I think she did this because it would have embarrassed her children, who had never taken the time to make gifts for their parents.

That night at supper, the Wheatleys thanked me for my gifts right after grace was offered. Mr. Wheatley gave a little talk about how enterprising I was to have made the gifts without notice, while keeping my chores done. The glow of praise was quickly cooled as Nathaniel tapped on his glass, meaning that I had better immediately pour his drink. With that, the whole routine of wait-ing table started and did not stop until we cleared the dishes away, so Mr. and Mrs. Wheatley could enjoy an after-dinner cup of tea. Chloe and I stayed at the table to take care of the Wheatleys, while the other slaves washed and put away the dishes. It would be our job to strip the dirty tablecloth, and sweep and clean the dining room. Before retiring, Mrs. Wheatley told me she had a special job for me tomorrow.

Early the next morning, I was sent to town on an errand. When I got home, I saw the dining table spread with tea and crumpets. Both Nathaniel and Mary were home. Nat had just returned from England, and Mary came all the way from Rhode Island. They were in Boston for the annual Wheatley family financial assessment that this year included considerable money paid them for my writing services.

For the past two years, I had been the head waitress for all culinary events during the family book balancing assemblage. I expected to wait on them again this year and was shocked when Nat and Mary invited me to sit at the big table.

I drank my first cup of tea that day. For some reason, the Wheatleys allowed none of their children to consume tea until their twelfth birthdays. They maintained the same rules for their slaves. It felt very strange sitting at the big table sipping tea. No other slave was treated like I was, and I knew, even as a twelve-year-old child, that I was treated well, because the Wheatleys expected to make a handsome sum selling my poems. With whispered encouragement from my slave friends, I relaxed and enjoyed the merriment. Other slaves later told me that they could feel my enjoyment inside themselves, even as they did their menial tasks.

The food and conversation were so good I actually forgot, for a brief period, that I was a slave. Then Mr. Wheatley excused himself and returned with a wrapped box that he presented to me. I told the family that, the first time they had given me a present, I'd thought the box itself was my gift and that I was shocked to discover that the gift was actually inside. This brought laughter from the Wheatley family.

I was careful not to say the words "birthday gift." I knew they still felt fearful about giving gifts on birthdays. I tore away the brown paper to reveal a plain box about the size of a book. I could not expect anything as nice as another book, I thought, as I gently opened the lid. Nestled inside was a book of Shakespeare's sonnets. With the Bible, and now Shakespeare, on my bookshelf, I was a very rich twelve-year-old who just happened to be a slave.

> *My children, suffer patiently*
> *the wrath that is come upon you from God:*
> *for thine enemy hath persecuted thee;*
> *but shortly thou shalt see his destruction,*
> *and shalt tread upon his neck.*
>
> Baruch 4:25

Chapter 6—Becoming a Woman

Ages 13—18

It seemed like just yesterday I celebrated my seventh birthday. I remember the talk that led to my being declared seven. Because I was so small, the Wheatleys wanted to make me younger than seven. I did not talk well and was a slave. I stood silent as seven became my given age. Using that first birthday as a benchmark today, April 15, 1766, I can say I am thirteen. As of today, I have served the Wheatley family for six years, but I also have been served, because I got to use their library, and they allowed me to write.

I was only thirteen, but often left by myself to watch over the house. The Wheatleys thought that the slaves might steal some of their valuables while they were away. I sensed trouble the minute I opened the door for Tom Carlyle, a friend of Nat's, but instead of telling Tom that Nat was not at home, I allowed—perhaps even encouraged—him to enter and sit in the parlor.

I wanted to be sociable, but I knew I could not socialize with Tom. Slaves did not associate with white people. Yet, something inside of me said Tom was a young man not much older than I, and nothing would be wrong if we talked. I longed to talk with him or any young man for that matter, so there I stood, not knowing what to do or say and wishing I had told Tom that the Wheatleys were not home.

Tom saw that we were alone, and he knew the Wheatleys would not return until tomorrow. Then he told me he had hidden his gold cuff links in the house during his visit the previous night. He said that unless I gave him the key to the silver cabinet, he would accuse me of stealing the cuff links and the silver pitcher he wanted. He told me that if I cooperated with him, he would give me a forty dollar bill, an amount that seemed like a small fortune.

Mr. Revere made the silver pitcher for my mistress, and I had never seen another quite as beautiful. I could understand why Tom would do anything to get it. Something I call my "knower" was screaming inside me not to take part in this evil scheme. I also knew that any slave accused of stealing was usually hanged without a trial.

Tom thought he had set a perfect trap and would emerge from the Wheatley home with the prized silver pitcher. I faced the ugly reality of trying to explain its disappearance. Tom told me that the Wheatleys were so rich that they would just accept its loss and wouldn't suspect their favorite slave of stealing. He never expected what happened next.

Slaves were not given any time to talk with one another. We worked often to the point of exhaustion and then slept, because our day started before sunrise, but there was just a little time after our owners went to bed and we had done all of our chores that we could spend together in the slave quarters. We were exhausted but took the time to create and practice a common African language. We could talk safely with each other in the presence of white people who thought we were just making noises. So when I stood by the window making loud noises, Tom thought it was just an African reaction to fear. He did not know that I told two outside slaves to enter the parlor, stand by Tom, and wait for more information.

My slave friends did exactly as I asked. Without knocking, they entered the parlor and stood beside Tom like bookends. In African, I explained to the slaves Tom's intentions and then in plain English I said to him,

"Two can play your game, Mr. Carlyle. Leave this house peacefully, sir, or we will throw you out. Furthermore, if you ever try to use me or any slave on this property again for your evil intentions, you will pay dearly. For example, if you don't leave peacefully today, your head will be cracked and your body stomped by a horse. We will tell anyone who asks that your horse threw you just as you approached the front gate. Have we made ourselves clear, Mr. Carlyle?"

With two strong African slaves at his side, Tom Carlyle made the right choice. Surprisingly, he told us how ashamed he was of his scheme for trying to steal the silver. Then he did not know how to say what he wanted to say next. He muttered the words, "I hurt you."

Tom knew he hurt us, but he also did not consider us worthy of an apology, because we were just slaves. He did not say anything else about hurting. He promised not even to think about taking someone else's property, but added the words "especially from my friends," which, in my mind, left an opening to take things from people not considered friends. We both agreed he could earn enough money to buy his own Revere pitcher, so there was no need to steal. Then he looked at me with a strange expression on his face. He was confiding in me, a slave, and he had feelings for me. He stopped talking and started crying. My slave friends had become uncomfortable and asked if they could leave. Tom was astonished that these Africans had such good English and that they still treated him with any respect. As they were leaving, they heard Tom, through his tears, tell me with no uncertainty that he was so sorry for trying to use me.

There was no doubt that Tom's disgrace gave way to a newfound humility. He told me how happy he was that we stopped him from carrying out a dastardly deed, then fetched his own coat and headed for the door. I was following close behind him as he opened the door to leave. He stopped suddenly and turned to face me. I will never know if he planned this maneuver or not, but I could not avoid falling into his open arms. He gave me a hug which my slave friends, who were still in front of the house, could see. Just as quickly, he went outside, tipped his hat to my friends, mounted his horse, and rode away.

I hate slavery with every ounce of my being, but, practically speaking, I fared well after being bought by the Wheatleys, and Mrs. Wheatley had assured me of freedom on my twenty-first birthday, or in the event of her death. As much as I wanted freedom, I could not bear to think about my Mistress dying. I never knew the name of Mrs. Wheatley's illness. At times, she seemed ready for death, and then she would be healthy again. It was as if she was in charge of her own death and could not make up her mind when to go. During her last year of life, those times that she could get out of bed, we did things together as if we were sisters. In the process of taking care of all of her needs, I had become very close to Mrs. Wheatley, and she to me.

I had to act like an adult almost every moment since leaving the slave ship, and I did a good job of it. On the outside I was a little woman, but inside I was a little girl. I could never let the little girl show. The little girl in me cried herself to sleep thinking of her real parents, and kept a baby doll made from corn husks hidden in her room, but now that little girl was changing.

Even Mrs. Wheatley did not notice me blooming as I began the process of becoming a woman. Mary no longer lived at home or had the time to counsel me when she visited. Things worked out so that my friend could help me. Thinking back now, I could have no finer counselor.

Obour dressed well and spoke English fluently. She was polite and always had a radiant smile on her face. The Wheatleys treated her with the same respect they gave me. They allowed us to act like sisters and gave us time together after we finished the chores. Obour's wise counsel guided me into adulthood. She was only three years older than I was, and I wondered how she knew so much. At first, I thought she was manufacturing her answers to my many questions. The Wheatley library did not have the books I needed to verify Obour's responses.

Obour served a doctor. I served a business person. She heard medical talk, and I heard business talk. Like me, she learned much from focused listening. We could not ask questions or even show an interest in non-slave talk. Also, we could not leave our master's sides, so someone usually asked what we wanted to ask. Both of our masters made us be with them as they carried on their business. Obour and I were blessed with good memories. Our masters felt comfortable talking around us because they did not think we were listening to them. A slave would be punished severely for listening to a master's conversation. We had to act like we did not hear their words—but then, to avoid hours of boredom, we listened.

I was standing at my master's side during one of his buys when I started my monthly bleeding. I had no idea what was happening to me. I remembered the fear caused by my almost forgotten coughing attacks. I did not tell my master my problem then or now, for fear of being sold. I thought that I was cursed because of the few seconds I had considered cooperating with Tom Carlyle. For that brief, uneasy moment, I considered going along with Tom, I would slowly bleed to death.

With much reluctance, I confided to Obour that I was dying. I explained that every month I bled from my private place because God punished me or I was cursed. I was shocked when my heartfelt revelation resulted in Obour laughing until tears came to her eyes. How could my best friend laugh at my seemingly certain early death?

Obour stopped laughing and looked at me with a serious expression on her face. She told me that I needed to listen to what she had to say without interrupting her, but she would answer my questions later. What she told me was so fascinating that it kept me silent even though I did have many questions to ask. Soon, I understood how ignorance of my own body had caused Obour to laugh, then get very serious.

I felt a deep concern for the thousands of young women in the same predicament as me, but without a friend like Obour. As Obour talked about conception, I took a silent vow to never bear a child while still a slave. I had a very powerful urge for motherhood—but an even greater desire for freedom.

*I will lift up mine eyes unto the hills,
from whence cometh my help.
My help cometh from the LORD,
which made heaven and earth.*

Psalm 121:1, 2

Chapter 7—Heaven Help Us

Mrs. Wheatley began to spend many hours in bed. Even though I knew who she was, the sight of her scared me. She looked like a ghost with her head peeping out from under the covers and white hair poking out from a ghastly bonnet. Bright red rouge colored her prominent cheekbones, made even more obvious because not eating had shrunk her face and made them stand out even more. A protester until the end, Mrs. Wheatley waited until her deathwatch to violate a religious code and wear rouge in a flawed attempt to look better on her death bed. The throes of death no doubt produced this one last effort to evade the obvious.

My mistress looked just like the evil spirits I imagined when I listened to scary ghost stories in my African village. I now know the storytellers made evil spirits hideous so children would avoid evil in our lives. I felt the effects of the storyteller's ability on each visit to Mrs. Wheatley's room.

At age thirteen, I was responsible for much of the household shopping. I even bought many of the Wheatleys' personal things. Mr. Wheatley was so busy that he often asked me to buy his personal things, and Mrs.

Wheatley was becoming too frail to shop. To keep me from socializing on shopping trips, they made me follow a strict time schedule. I had absolutely no time for myself and always had to rush to get shopping done. If I was just a little bit late, I was accused of socializing. There was no acceptable excuse, and I had to endure false accusations every week of my slave life. I was never punished, but I know of many slave beatings as a result of a suspicion of socialization.

One day, I had to take the wagon to town for repair. The Wheatleys knew I would spend many hours waiting for the job to be completed, so they advised me to read the Bible and forbade my going anywhere except the livery stable. For nourishment, I was allowed to take some crumpets and a flask of water. The repair took much longer than anticipated, and I was famished. I envied the people who were free to buy a meal and avoid the pangs of hunger.

Luckily for me, the old slave who knew me entered the livery with a pail of food. He was there to buy a horse. Also, the livery was one of the few places in town that allowed slaves a place to sit down and eat. He had better food than I did, and he gladly shared his lunch. He told me a story that I later learned was about how he became a free man. He did this to encourage me because he knew I needed more than just food to rejuvenate.

He started by correcting my thinking about his being a slave. He told me he worked on a whaling ship, having escaped slavery about seventeen years ago. It took him almost a year to get to Boston, and he nearly lost his life in the process. Strange that I assumed every African was a slave.

Before beginning his story, my friend had one more important detail to tell me. He had tried to tell me the last time we met, but I did not give him the chance. In a deep, resonant voice, he said,

"My name is Crispus Attucks, but my friends call me Tuck."

He asked me in a nice polite way to call him "Tuck." I felt so bad that I'd been so taken with his adulation of me at our first meeting that I forgot to get his name. I told Tuck how much I appreciated being his friend and tried not to reveal how I really felt. Somehow Tuck sensed my shame. In that wonderful, soothing voice he said,

"Miss Wheatley, I know you were under pressure when we first met, and I imposed on you, but I'm thankful you have the time to hear my story today."

Then he began the story of the escape from slavery that nearly cost him his life. At dusk on the first day of his escape, a combination of darkness and his haste caused him to step near a large snake. He heard the horrible rattle of the vicious viper as it got away by crawling through a field of wild wheat. He could no longer see it, but the wheat continued to be parted as if a small log was being pulled through it.

He had to walk the backwoods in order to avoid bounty hunters looking for escaped slaves. Crispus knew the odds for living in the rough country were not much better than using the good roads. All he had for guidance were the sun and stars, and nature provided his nourishment. Nature also nearly took his life.

Tuck entered a small cave to get some relief from the hot sun. He walked just a few steps, and then, neck high, a huge rattlesnake unleashed a potentially lethal strike on the unsuspecting intruder. The buzz was so close to his ear that it startled Tuck. At the same time, he recognized his precarious predicament. The snake had no retreat and so struck Tuck with a full load of hot venom right in the neck.

Tuck told me he swelled from head to toe and felt excruciating pain. He remembered a funny taste in his mouth right before mercifully passing out. He also knew he was dead.

Then, according to Tuck, a strange, good feeling overwhelmed him. He recalled floating above the trees and looking down on his bloated body. He could also see that no one was tracking him and that the serpent assailant was crawling across his grotesque body as it left the cave.

Tuck told me that he floated higher and higher until he was sucked into the center of a tunnel not much bigger than his body. Once inside the tunnel, he moved very fast. Everything became blurry, the way things look when you're riding a fast horse. His eyes focused on a spot of light at the end of the tunnel that got increasingly larger as he got closer to it. He flew into the light, and it was so bright that at first he could not see. His eyesight came back quickly, but with awesome power of sight.

He found himself in a beautiful garden surrounded by the largest, most colorful flowers he had ever seen. Also, he simply felt warm and at peace. Someone, he's not sure who, approached him and, when his light engulfed Tuck's body, Tuck saw his entire life flow before him. He felt badly when he saw himself do something wrong in his life review. During those bad scenes of his life, the light-being comforted him. The light-being let Tuck know that he had to see his many mistakes, but gave him the power to tolerate the sight. Tuck also knew that he had done more good than harm and that he would return to earth to complete an unknown, but very important, task.

Tuck did not want to return to the misery of earth and begged to stay in the garden. However, he soon gave in and said he would return to earth. At once, he left the garden and was back inside the cave. He awoke with a swollen, painful body and just a vague memory of the beautiful garden. Tuck lay there unable to move, praying for sleep and wondering what task required him to leave paradise and return to such suffering.

Sleep finally came, and Tuck began a therapeutic coma lasting many days. He was awakened by a bright noon sun engulfing the cave entrance. At first, he thought he was dead. Then he pulled himself to his feet and staggered down to a nearby creek to quench an unbelievable thirst. He gulped water into a parched mouth despite the presence of a most unpleasant taste. He told me that it took months for the bad taste to go away, and it occasionally returns when he drinks or eats something very hot.

Tuck ended his story still wondering about the important task he was sent back to Earth to accomplish. He gave me the following warning:

"Whatever you do, Miss, don't do no harm, because you're only hurting yourself. Also, do as much good as possible, because it makes up for the bad things we do."

Finally, Tuck's face almost shone as he said, "You and I will be in a much better place than this someday. I don't have the words to tell you about it. Only thing I knows, I want to go there as soon as possible, and I want all my friends, especially you, to be there with me."

After Tuck finished his story, he just sat there in a daze, staring into space with the most peaceful look on his face. The liveryman's gruff voice startled him back to reality with the impudent announcement:

"This is the best horse I can sell to a black man."

Tuck had to pay twice the value for an old horse and worn-out saddle, but he just smiled, paid the bill, and thanked the man. He told me that he was going to spend some time on dry ground because, he was tired of life at sea. He wanted to find a cottage and grow a garden. He expected abuse, but said he could now tolerate anything, just by calling to mind the vision of the garden. He wished me well and rode away in pursuit of a dream.

To the students at the University of Cambridge in New England:

Improve your privileges while they stay,
Ye pupils, and each hour redeem, that bears
Or good or bad report of you to heav'n.

Phillis Wheatley

Chapter 8—Teaching Prejudice

Soon after Tuck left, the liveryman announced the completion of Mr. Wheatley's repairs. I was not sure his call was for Mr. Wheatley's carriage and waited for him to make another call. He chose to come over to the Negro section and shout his message so loud I'm sure the people on the next block heard him.

I could say nothing about how I was dealt with, because I was a slave, and slaves had no rights. All I could do was hand over the money. The liveryman accepted cash from my black hands, but his hate provided a bargain for Mr. Wheatley. The bill was more than the estimate, and Mr. Wheatley gave me cash in the exact amount of the estimate. Rather than talk with me, the liveryman crossed out the higher amount and took the money Mr. Wheatley had given me to pay for the repairs. I watched carefully as he marked the bill "Paid in Full." I was thankful that he wrote "paid" on the bill, because I did not want to go through the process of tricking him into marking the bill paid. I wanted to tell him that I would bring the rest of the money the next day. I chose to say nothing, to see if the liveryman would say something to me. Rather than talk to me, he immediately left his desk and threw the receipt at me.

Dealing with hatred made me angry, but I could not show that anger for fear of punishment. It is a shame that the liveryman's pride kept him from asking for the correct sum. He looked like he needed every penny he could get. If one could account for all the money lost because of prejudice, I have no doubt that the sum would be quite large.

One of my favorite African stories would fit nicely here, so I will share a bit of Mother Africa with you. Our village had several storytellers. Most often just called tellers, they not only kept us amused, but also taught us how to behave. In Africa, stories are not just told but acted out by costumed tellers. They charmed everyone with their tales from sunrise until sunrise. Yes, you could be enchanted at any time of the day or night, every day. We were much richer than Americans were.

Some of the best stories were the spooky ones told after midnight, but the one I am going to tell is a simple daytime story. I can remember making the decision to love everyone after I heard the story for the first time. The two main characters are Boy Frog and Boy Snake, and I'll do my best to recall all the details.

One day, a little Boy Frog happened upon a long, shiny creature that introduced himself as Boy Snake. This was Boy Frog's first trip away from his birthplace, and he enjoyed bouncing along on his newly grown legs. Boy Snake said to Boy Frog,

"That sure looks fun. How do you jump like that?"

Boy frog said, "I'll be happy to show you, but we'll have to make some adaptations."

They both talked about how Boy Frog jumped and together figured out that if Boy Snake stuck his tail in the mud and folded his long body against his tail, he could spring forward like his frog friend. They played "jump" until they were so exhausted they could only lie in the sun with their tongues hanging out. As they recovered their energy, both noticed that they had very different tongues. Immediately, they started a conversation about these very neat appendages. During the discussion, they discovered how much they both liked red ants, but they ate them in very different ways. Boy Snake had to crawl right into the middle of the anthill to capture the delicious morsels, and that often led to rather severe ant bites. Boy Frog could stand way back and capture ants with his long, sticky tongue, but had a very difficult time finding the ants.

Talking about red ants made both of them very hungry for this special treat. Boy Snake impressed Boy Frog by flicking his tongue out very fast and sensing red ants right on the other side of a little hill. Boy Frog climbed the hill, and sure enough he looked right down on a huge anthill. Boy Frog sat on the hill snapping up vast amounts of red ants, which he generously shared with his friend. Teamwork resulted in plenty of food with no painful ant stings. Boy Snake was so happy he instinctively slithered up a tall tree and wrapped himself around a limb, then realized Boy Frog was still down on the ground. Boy Snake quickly descended the tree and apologized for being so rude. Boy Frog said,

"No need to apologize; just teach me how you did that."

Following Boy Snake's careful instructions, Boy Frog extended his front and hind legs tightly together, and, controlling muscles he never knew he had, he was able to slither up a small tree with the snake. The view was spectacular, as they clung lazily to the gently rocking branches. They played together until the sun began to set, at which time they parted company with the unspoken promise to play together tomorrow.

Boy Frog arrived home by slithering the last several feet. Upon seeing her son crawling on his belly, Mother Frog bellowed, "And just where did you learn to move like a stupid snake?"

Boy Frog was shocked that his mother referred to his new friend as stupid. Boy Frog told his mother that he played with Boy Snake all day and wanted to play with him tomorrow. His mother told him that frogs don't associate with snakes and that snakes had poison teeth they used to kill frogs. She admonished him never to hobnob with snakes again, or he would end up dead.

Boy Snake arrived home using the newly learned springing method just taught him by his friend Boy Frog. Snake's mother saw her son moving like a frog and proceeded to berate him for such outlandish behavior. She harshly told her son that he looked like a frog, and snakes should never act like such low-life. She asked him where he learned to behave in such a ridiculous way, and Boy Snake told her about his new friend Boy Frog.

Boy Snake's mother told her son that snakes eat frogs. Further, if Boy Frog gets close to him again, Boy Snake should strike the frog with his open mouth and then wrap his long, muscular body tightly around the frog until the frog stops breathing. The mother explained to Boy Snake that snakes are superior to frogs and that frogs deserve whatever punishment snakes can inflict on them.

Both Boy Snake and Boy Frog had a very difficult time sleeping that night. They respected their mothers, but an inner voice kept them awake, trying to correct all the misinformation given to them by their mothers. Following their advice would eliminate any possibility of the friendship they both craved. The boys slept poorly, and they both approached the next day tired and full of anxiety. Both experienced nightmares in which they followed the dictums of their mothers. The nightmares caused both of them to awake dripping with sweat and in great remorse.

At breakfast, both got yet another stern warning from their respective parents to avoid or, in the case of snake, do injury to someone who only yesterday was a friend. Frog started hopping down the path, but today he was full of fear that a snake would be right around the next corner. Snake slithered down the path conjuring up all the mean things he could do to a frog if one happened to appear.

Deep down, both the frog and the snake did not want to see each other. Boy Frog believed his mother, but just could not imagine his snake friend hurting him. Boy Snake was prepared to hurt any unsuspecting frog he happened on, except the one special frog who'd taught him to spring.

Very soon their paths crossed, just like the day before. Only this time, Boy Frog kept a good distance from Boy Snake, which was difficult to do because Boy Snake kept moving toward Boy Frog. They seemed to be doing a circular dance to some soundless, enchanting music. Because they were very tense, they both tired quickly and moved to some lily pads and an old floating log. They could not get close to one another, and both had to keep one eye always open and focused on the old friend, now a mortal enemy. Their mistrust and hatred prevented any form of communication.

That is the way Mr. Frog and Mr. Snake behave today. They spend all day sitting around, making sure to keep their distance from one another. Frogs have forgotten how to slither, and snakes no longer move by springing. Just for meanness, snakes spring to bite, especially when they bite frogs. They spend their time hating each other and have no memory of that one special day of friendship.

I just told you one of my favorite African stories. It explained for me the reason I saw frogs and snakes lounging on the lily pads and logs of Blue Lake, but never very close to one another. However, I intuitively knew that the story had a deeper meaning, a meaning that left me profoundly puzzled, and I often requested this story in search of that deeper meaning.

The reason that I could not figure out the moral was that our mother did not teach us to hate anyone. Slavery over-powered me with unexplainable hatred. How could anybody hate people, just because they were different? I have tried to describe being treated like an animal, but now I realize the situation is even worse.

In Africa, we used animals for food, work, and friendship. We only harvested what we needed, and we took care of all injured beasts, releasing them as soon as they recovered. So even though we used animals, we also had much respect for them. We knew how important they were for our existence and that our lives were directly connected to theirs.

Now I know that Americans will not even treat slaves with the dignity we bestow on animals in Africa. I often saw children, for example, delivering maiming blows to adult slaves simply for amusement. Slaves are non-humans, non-animals—in a class by ourselves, subject to abuse at the whim of any free American.

[The Lord says,]
...yet will I not forget thee.
Behold, I have graven thee
upon the palms of my hands....

Isaiah 49:15b-16

Chapter 9—Free at Last

I wrote to clear the thoughts swimming in my head and out of the sheer joy of the process. The idea that some of my work might survive beyond my brief stay on earth encouraged me. My mistress got many requests for my writing, and that attention also fueled my endeavors—though, to be honest, many of those requests stemmed from the novelty of a literate slave rather than from the quality of my work.

Watching courageous colonists get ready for war day and night moved me to write some of my best poetry. On the other hand, I wondered how they could be so desirous of their own freedom, while at the same time enslaving Africans. Why couldn't the colonists see their treatment of Africans was worse than any British tax? How could they go to war over money while engaging in the practice of buying and selling human beings?

Writing poems about a possible war made me famous in the Boston area. Bostonians had no idea of how to deal with a slave poetess. At dinners and parties, I usually sat at a separate table or section of the room, often kept in isolation until it was time for me to read my poetry. Worse, many times people's racism was revealed, and they would openly say that I could not write at all—much less create such beautiful poetry. In those instances, I delighted in creating a poem in front of everyone. I asked the most bigoted person to suggest the topic and a volunteer to write down the words as I said them aloud. I ended by giving the poem to the bigot as a keepsake. That tactic always silenced the disbelievers, but even after my writing skills became well-known, I did not get the same recognition as white poets.

Mrs. Wheatley, perhaps feeling some guilt, established a bank account in my name. She never told me how much of the money I was paid for my poetry that I got to keep, and I was not allowed to know how much was in the account, but at least, I enjoyed yet another privilege unknown to most slaves—a personal bank account. Being allowed to keep a small portion of the money I received for my work was another inducement to write.

Nat came home from his business trip to England full of excitement. I thought it was because of his engagement to his English lady friend, but to my surprise, the prospect of making a lot of money by publishing my poetry in England caused his exhilaration. A bound copy of my work had found its way into the home of the Huntingdon family, and they wanted to sponsor the book for London publication.

Mrs. Wheatley tried to get my poems published in Boston and Philadelphia. She told me that every publisher who read my poetry wanted to print it until they found out I was black. She could not find a publisher willing to print a book written by a black woman. No matter how hard she tried, she could not convince book publishers that my writing was not a hoax.

Mrs. Wheatley asked for help from a minister friend and managed to get a publisher to agree to print my book, if three more supporters could be found. She made a valiant effort, but could not find even one person willing to help finance a publication by a slave. While his mother was not meeting with success in attempts to get my work published, things were very different for Nat in England.

The Huntingdons told Nat that they wanted to meet me, and they would gladly pay my expenses to England. Nat made arrangements to take me along on his next trip to England, and the Huntingdons paid for my first-class ticket. I was thrilled, but I wondered why Nat was taking such an interest in me after all these years of treating me as just another servant. I concluded that, like his parents, he saw my potential income as more important than my service.

I think Mrs. Wheatley knew that I was going to become important in England. I had become well-known in the Boston area, but I was also shunned because I was a slave. Somehow, Mrs. Wheatley sensed that the British had a different attitude toward Africans. She probably got that impression from listening to Nat's many descriptions of life in England. England outlawed slavery and gave former slaves the respect due any human being. I cannot tell you how good it felt to be considered human. Yes, my work would sell well in Great Britain.

The English made good use of the fact that Bostonians had all but rejected me because of my color. One of their reasons for going to war with the colonies was that colonists abused Africans. The British cited me as a typical slave. Of course, nothing could have been farther from the truth, but I went along with the ploy because I thought it might help the anti–slavery movement. After the war started, I realized that the Wheatley home was in the center of the battle zone. I had to wonder if the friendliness of the British toward the Wheatleys had something to do with English war plans. I dismissed that thought because, in my view, the British did very little planning for their battles with the colonists.

Mrs. Wheatley's health was so bad she knew death's visit was imminent. As sick as she was, she insisted that I go with Nat to England. She knew my trip to England might result in a profitable book deal. Even the British suspected that I could not be a real writer, and she knew that personal contact with me would quickly dispatch such thoughts.

The last time I had sailed the ocean I had been chained below the deck as "black gold." On this voyage, even though I partook of luxury, I awoke in the middle of night in a cold sweat, mentally imprisoned in the filthy hold of a slave ship. The sound of waves hitting the side of the ship reminded me of being chained inside the *Louisa*. Terror overtook me in my sleep as my heart beat against my chest. Embarrassment followed as my scream awakened me, but I was thankful that I did not wake anyone else.

For a frightful few moments, as I sat on the edge of my bed, I could feel someone pushing me toward the hold of the slave ship. For some reason, I covered my face, and when I did, realty began to return. I realized that it had been a nightmare, and that I was in fact traveling first-class to London. I looked around the cabin. Then I knew the thick planks and lush drapery had muted my screams. Fatigue and fear rather than sleepiness put me back to sleep. For the first time in my life, I slept until mid-morning, and arose still unsure of myself.

On the voyage, I used none of my meager funds, because the Huntingdons took care of all my expenses, but my past, and the reality of being the only dark-skinned person on the ship, enslaved me. I knew we were sailing over the bones of thousands of my African compatriots.

It was very difficult to remain seated and not serve people, especially master Nathaniel. I had taken care of him for nearly eight years and just did not feel right not reacting to his needs. All of the ship's servants were white, so there was no way to avoid having a white person wait on me. Nat saw my discomfort and moved his chair next to mine and put his arm around me. Then I truly did not know what to do. I just sat there with a forced smile on my face.

Help came when a well-dressed lady came over to our table and politely asked me if I would recite some of my poetry. She knew I was the slave poet and apologized for bothering me. Nat looked perplexed as I gently moved his arm and got up to accept the lady's invitation. I had some notice in Boston, but nothing compared to what I got from my fellow travelers, and I was totally unprepared for the attention Nat was giving me.

After supper the next day, I read poetry for almost two hours and then stayed in the hall to answer questions. That night, the Captain and I made an agreement for a show every Monday, Wednesday, and Saturday night. I would have worked for free, but the Captain insisted on paying me a sum of money that astounded me.

You could not have convinced me that my treatment in England would be superior to what I received on board ship, but, from the moment the ship docked, I was treated like royalty. The English love poets, and the novelty of a young, slave poet made me the center of attention.

The day I arrived in England, the king and queen were setting sail for France, and I was unable to have an audience with them. My benefactors assured me that my next visit would be timed so I would meet the royal family. I was flattered that they wanted to see me, but I was more thrilled by the prospect of another visit to England than by encountering the nobility. My mother and father, after all, were royalty, so I knew the king and queen were just ordinary people.

One of the highlights of my trip to England was the attention given me by Benjamin Franklin, who happened to be in England during my visit. When he found out I was there, he invited me to his London hotel, and we spent the entire day together. It turned out that Mr. Franklin and I shared a mutual admiration for the British preacher named George Whitefield. Mr. Franklin was very taken by the elegy I wrote for the Rev. Whitefield's funeral. During one of our talks about Rev. Whitefield, Mr. Franklin told me how much he hated slavery, but he said he was afraid slavery would be part of America for a long time after his death.

Bad news arrived on our sixth week in England. Nat got word from the captain of a cargo ship that his mother was near death, and she wanted us to return immediately. The only fast way to return home was as an employee on a cargo ship. The next passenger ship would not leave for two weeks.

Nat made a tough decision. He was engaged to an English lady. He decided to stay in England, so he could finish getting ready for his wedding. He would take the passenger ship home in two weeks. He told me that he somehow knew his mother would not die until he got home. He booked me on the cargo ship that was setting sail the next morning.

It was probably best that I did not return home as a pampered passenger because I had to go back to being a slave. Working on a cargo ship better prepared me to resume my slave life. The unfair and abusive conduct I faced daily on my return trip was just like the behavior I dealt with as a slave. I was still spared much abuse because of the reputation of Master Wheatley, however, and I thought it remarkable that even on the high seas being a slave of Master Wheatley gave me some protection. Nat had no idea of how strenuous the work would be on a cargo ship. It would have been very rude to expect payment of my return ticket from the Huntingdons after such a brief and unproductive visit. The Huntingdons tried to pay, but Nat made it clear that it was not, under the circumstances, their responsibility. I know that Nat would not have worked on a cargo ship, but expected it of me. My concern for Mrs. Wheatley, and the knowledge that this was truly the only way home for the next two weeks, mandated my acceptance of the job.

The night before I was to leave England, Nat came to my room. He told me that he wanted to talk about how I was going to explain to his mother his not returning to Boston with me. I really did not want to talk with him, because I thought he should go home and be with his dying mother. It seemed to me that pleasure now controlled Nat, making being his slave even more difficult. I knew that he would ask me to be less than truthful about why he did not come home, but he was my Master's son, which meant that he owned me. You do not tell the person who owns you to leave.

The Wheatleys had never taken advantage of any slave that I know about. In particular, I was always treated properly. I was very thankful that Mr. Wheatley did not use an overseer, because they could be cruel to slaves. Also, I had escaped being branded, so I was not disfigured like many slaves I knew. So, I felt an obligation to be kind to Master Nathaniel.

Instead of talking about his absence, Nat started talking about his future. I felt uncomfortable, just as I did the time Tom Carlyle tried to steal the silver pitcher while the Wheatleys were away. I did not want to judge Nat's intentions. Rather, I held the thought that Nat did not know what he was doing. I was not the person to ask about married life, and I did not feel comfortable talking about love with the son of my owners.

I politely told Nat that I could not help him with his concerns about being married. Then I suggested that we pray together for help from above. Nat agreed, and we both got on our knees and asked the Lord to be with us in a special way during the next few weeks. At first, Nat seemed to be just saying words, but then beautiful thoughts began to pour from his heart, and I knew his prayers were sincere. Finally, he looked me straight in the eyes, and said,

"Louisa, we are very different, but we have the same God. Thank you for reminding me about our God."

We both got up, and Nat went immediately to the door. Before he left, he told me that he knew I would say the right words to his mother.

Although I had not done much work, I was very tired. The time I'd spent with Nat drained me of all my energy. I packed all my belongings in a special traveling chest made for me by a talented slave cabinet-maker. The next morning, it was as if I had not slept at all that night, and boarding the cargo ship seemed like part of dream. The dream did not last long, as the captain ordered me to have a meal ready for the men as soon as we left the harbor and the sailing was smooth.

Like everyone else on board, I worked 12 hours a day, mostly washing clothes and cooking. Keeping the men's stomachs full and clothes clean made them less irritable and rude. Working hard also assured me of sound sleep. Not one person on board the cargo ship was interested in poetry or literature.

For my protection, the Captain allowed me to lodge in a storage closet near his room. Just enough space was cleared to provide me a bed. As much as possible, the Captain watched over me during the day. Still, the leering eyes of hardened sailors kept me unnerved and under great tension. I looked forward to the protection of the

Wheatley home, even though I would have to comfort Mrs. Wheatley. It would also be left to me to explain why Nat did not immediately return to America.

With great reluctance, Mr. Wheatley chose to drive the carriage himself to pick up his son and his slave. Mrs. Wheatley had been unconscious the entire day before I arrived, and Mr. Wheatley did not want to leave his wife's side. The doctor convinced him that Mrs. Wheatley's condition would not change during a brief trip to Boston Harbor. From the look on his face when he picked me up, he must have cried all the way to the harbor. I prayed silently that my Master would be able to bear the death of his beloved wife.

Mr. Wheatley was very sad when he met me at the dock. I hated to disturb him even more by telling him about Nat's decision to stay in England. When I told him it obviously brought him anguish, but then he said he simply could not be hurt any worse than by his wife's illness. He asked me not to talk about Nat any more.

I was relieved to disembark the cargo ship, where I had been made to work harder than any slave, and with only the Captain to protect me from the men on the ship, I had lived in fear during the entire trip. I recognized our buggy, but was shocked to see an unkempt and heartbroken Mr. Wheatley as the driver. He apologized for his appearance, explaining that he had not left his wife's bedside for three days. He cherished each moment Mrs. Wheatley returned from her coma to utter a few words or just exchange glances with him.

As we pulled away from the dock heading for home, he could no longer hold back his tears. No coherent sentences were exchanged between us as he whipped the horse into a fast pace. After we traveled a brief distance, he began to describe many memorable episodes in his married life. Then he suddenly stopped talking and deep, heartfelt cries of grief gushed forth. When the carriage came to a stop at the front door, I helped Mr. Wheatley out. He was barely able to walk, and once inside the house, he collapsed.

Another servant came to take care of Mr. Wheatley, and I went up to Mrs. Wheatley's room. I gently opened the door to discover the doctor bending over my comatose mistress, holding a small mirror in front of my lady's mouth. Soon, Mr. Wheatley came in, having regained his composure, but the servant stayed by his side in case he collapsed again.

Then the most unusual thing happened. Seemingly caught in the grasp of death, Mrs. Wheatley suddenly sat up in bed and, with great lucidity, said:

"Please listen to these my last words. I give Louisa her freedom. On my death, she will be free. John, please let her stay here until she is able to live on her own. I give Louisa $500, which should be put in a bank account for her on the day of my funeral. Louisa, please write a short, simple eulogy for my funeral. John, I'll be waiting for you."

She lay back down and, looking toward heaven she said, "Come quickly, sweet Jesus. Come quickly."

My mistress then took her last breath and left us. I can't believe that, for a brief moment, she appeared normal, and then slipped so quickly into the great beyond. Ever a proper lady, Mrs. Wheatley spared us all a grueling death-watch and made her last human act, dying, a most considerate occasion.

Mr. Wheatley did everything his wife asked of him on her death bed. I kept my little room and continued with my chores, all the while gradually using my new freedom. The slow, small changes I made to my life allowed both Mr. Wheatley and me to adjust to our new circumstances.

My main step into freedom was going to a pub that served as a meeting place for some of the more learned members of Boston society. Mr. Wheatley even allowed me to use a small buggy and never questioned me about my new life. Still, I maintained most of my servile work and left only at convenient times.

I was surprised when pub patrons gathered around my table to hear my poetry. I was dumbfounded when this audience presented me with a sizable sum of money for my performance. For the first time in my life, I got to keep every penny, because I was a free person. I wondered if they enjoyed my work or paid to see the peculiar phenomenon of a smart slave. The pub even displayed and sold my books. As my bank account grew, I began to think of moving into my own home.

I was still unable to get my books published in Boston. A respectable British publisher kept them stocked in London bookstores. With every royalty check, he would also send me a box of books to sell locally, taking a small deduction from the check for this service. The Boston booksellers bought my monthly ration of books from England. The local money I made combined with my royalty check from England gave me a sizeable income.

I set up another bank account and soon had enough money to separate totally from the Wheatley home. I rented a small bungalow near the pub. Mr. Wheatley gladly agreed to co-sign my rent papers, but I can proudly say that he never had to contribute any support. The next year, my landlord did not require a co-signer for my new lease, and I knew I was now independent.

One night, a handsome African came to the pub, and our eyes immediately made contact. Truthfully, contact was natural, since I was on a small stage reciting poetry. Still, I sensed that he was special. I watched out of the corner of my eye as this dark-skinned man was entreated to join a table near the stage. The people seemed very pleased that he chose to sit with them, even though he was black as coal. I read one more poem and then went to my usual booth, where my friends were waiting to talk. Then it occurred to me that I enjoyed the same acceptance as the mysterious black man.

We were talking about the likelihood of the colonies splitting away from the rule of England. I was engrossed in the discussion, except I had a feeling someone was standing near me. I looked up and saw the African standing politely beside me, waiting for a break in our conversation.

A slight under-the-table kick to my friend's shin caused her to stop talking long enough for the gentleman to introduce himself. Our eyes met again as he said,

"My name is John Peters, and I am so glad to finally get to hear your beautiful poetry. Everything I have heard about you is true."

A return kick from the friend resulted in the only words I could force from my frozen body: "Thank you."

Someone called Mr. Peters from across the room, and he graciously excused himself. Soon thereafter he and his friends left, and I feared that I would not see him again. I was so distraught that I left the pub early and spent the rest of the night trying to sleep. It was early morning before my mind relaxed, and I got, at the most, two hours of sleep.

Three days later, Mr. Peters returned to the pub. He came straight to my table and reintroduced himself by unabashedly calling himself "your admirer." I asked him to sit down, and we began visiting like we had known each other for years. I found out that John had been free for 10 years and made a good living as a landlord and lawyer. He told me that all of his clients were Africans, until recently, when he represented a white person involved in a property dispute. He easily won the case and predicted more white people would now hire him.

We both realized we had spent the last hour talking business without any socializing. We had to relax and learn to enjoy each other's company. John suggested we go to a play on Saturday and not allow ourselves to spend any time talking about our work. I agreed to go to the play with him, trying to act calm even though I was so excited I felt like screaming. We spent the rest of the evening together, and I can only remember thinking that my father must have been just like John when he was young. John walked me home and left promptly as I opened my door. His only words were,

"I will pick you up at six, my dear."

It took me a long time to fall asleep, as I thought about the night and about seeing John again next week. It seemed to take longer than usual for Saturday to arrive, but when John appeared at my door, I lost track of time. I do not remember the name of the play we saw, but I recall having to remind John not to talk about business. To be honest, he had to remind me several times. We laughed about the slip-ups when we found ourselves talking about work. We laughed at ourselves for being so concerned about paying bills. After the laugh, we both relaxed. I felt bliss like nothing I had ever known before. I longed to share my feelings with Obour, but my only friend lived too far away.

Awakening on Sunday, I knew I wanted to marry John Peters. I wondered if he felt the same way about me, and how long would it take for him to ask for my hand. My answer came quickly. Following a knock on my door, I opened it to find John on my porch with an astonished look on his face. Considerable time passed before he began speaking.

John stuttered, probably for the first time in his life, as he asked me to walk with him to the corner coffeehouse. I agreed and quickly freshened myself while John browsed through my small library. We left my little cottage hand in hand, and I felt like we were the only two people on earth.

Walking to the coffeehouse, I felt so secure with his strong hand holding mine. We entered the coffee-house, and John picked a table for two at the back. He ordered coffee and sweet rolls, getting exactly what I wanted without asking me. We sat looking into each other's eyes, and then John leaned across the table and whispered,

"I love you."

This was not the first time he had said those words, but it was the most memorable. The next words out of his mouth were,

"Louisa, will you marry me?"

I said "yes" so fast that I was embarrassed. John whispered a polite "Thank you," and then we both just sat there looking into each other's eyes. Neither of us saw the waiter standing politely beside us with our food. Both of us were crying tears of joy when we finally saw him. As the waiter put the food on the table, I noticed that he also had tears streaming down his face. At that moment, everyone in the little coffeehouse started clapping for us. I felt more joy than I had ever known in my life, but deep inside there was also concern.

He that handleth a matter wisely shall find good: and whoso trusteth in the LORD, happy is he.

Proverbs 16:20

Chapter 10 – Two Unforgettable Events

New Freedom and Responsibility

I wanted to marry John as soon as possible, but living with the Wheatley family for so many years left me with many of their traits. I could hear Mr. Wheatley saying, "Time is capital. Invest it wisely."

Although I knew John was the right man for me, I also knew not to rush into such an important event as marriage. Still, I was surprised at myself as I said the words, "John, our love will easily endure a delay in our marriage plans."

His expression told me he was deeply hurt, but he did not interrupt me or show anger. I watched silently as he tried to hide his pain, and I felt anguish at the thought that I had wounded him. I deeply desired to be married to this remarkable man, but besides trying to avoid a hasty choice of life mate, I also had an unfinished ode dwelling in my heart. The concentration needed to complete a timely revolutionary ode cooled the forge of love that would eventually meld our hearts.

After talking all morning and into the night, we both thought it best for me to finish the writing task that was taking so much of my time. We both wanted children, and

John knew I could not write and take care of children at the same time. His would be the only family income until the children were up in years, so we agreed to give each other more time. I would finish my ode to Washington, and John would practice law and manage property. John was prone to starting one business venture after the next and often lost money in the process. Law and real estate were his most consistent and profitable sources of income, and he told me he would concentrate on those two things and do them as well as he could. We had helped each other, and the future seemed most inviting.

General Washington came to Boston for a secret meeting. It took place at the Wheatley Wharf, and I was there to serve the fifty or so men attending. I overheard the men talking about destroying a shipload of British tea just a few years back. They talked about how a few members tried to put tea in their pockets and had to be stopped. They laughed about beating the floating bags of tea with their oars to sink the stuff. Until the night of the meeting, I thought Mohawk Indians had made the raid on the three British ships in Boston Harbor. Very funny to me was the fact that I was at the meeting for the sole purpose of serving tea to those present. Mr. Wheatley let everyone know that the tea was from old stock that had to be used due to its age. These men loved their tea, so it must have been very difficult to destroy so much and then carry out the tea boycott. No one questioned Mr. Wheatley's explanation, and they kept me busy keeping their cups full.

In late 1775, I often saw Washington walking past the Wheatley home. He was always dressed in regular clothes and looked just like all the other residents of Boston. I found out at another planning meeting that during these walks he was checking the troops, who were also dressed in regular clothes. On one particular day, General Washington happened upon a man I later learned was a Second Lieutenant in the new colonial army. The Lieutenant was in charge of what looked like the repair of the road leading down to Boston Harbor. He had never met Washington and did not know what he looked like.

The shoulders on both sides of the road were being reinforced with large, flat rocks. Trails were made through the thick undergrowth back to the open forest. It looked like the men were repairing the road, but instead they were making trails and protection for the local minutemen. The rocks could be turned on their sides to shield sharpshooters from British fire. At that time, the colonies did not have an official army, but the men could rally within minutes whenever they heard the church bells ring. The plan was to give the colonial army easy shots at the British troops as they came across a narrow river bridge. Then our troops could make a hasty retreat into the nearby protective forest. It took many meetings to prepare these plans, and I served tea at every one of them. No one questioned Mr. Wheatley's vast supply of "old" tea.

Back to my story about the Lieutenant who had just barked orders to the men to move faster. I saw General Washington, out on his daily inspection, stop and watch this group of men closely. I stepped out on the front porch just in time to hear the General ask the officer why he was not doing any of the work. The officer told Washington that he was the boss, and bosses did not do the hard work. He said that his job was to make sure the men did everything right. Washington asked the Lieutenant if the job had to be done by a certain time. The Lieutenant said that the job had to be done today, because most of the men had to be somewhere else tomorrow.

General Washington volunteered to work with the troops and spent the next five hours doing hard manual labor. By dark the work was finished, and the Lieutenant called the men together. This was done so they could end the day with some semblance of military protocol. The Lieutenant asked the stranger, whom he knew only by his first name of George, to join the group. The young officer wanted to thank the hard-working stranger in front of the men. He praised the man he knew as George for giving his time to help fix the road and asked him if he wanted to join the crew. General Washington was glad that at no time during the day could you tell that the road work was really a military action. Also, he was pleased that the Lieutenant had not asked him to join the militia, because he could have been a British spy. Imagine how the Lieutenant and the men felt after the stranger named George told them his full name. Everybody came to attention and General Washington quickly told them to be at ease. He then said this to the group:

"Anytime there is hard work that must be done, you can count on me for help. I will always do whatever is necessary for the good of this great country."

I thought of General Washington helping his troops prepare for war as I wrote:

"Or thick as leaves in Autumn's golden reign,
Such, and so many, moves the warrior's train.
In bright array they seek the work of war,
Where high unfurl'd the ensign waves in air.
Shall I to Washington their praise recite?"

Thinking about the strong character of Washington caused words to flow from my quill like the song of a spring robin. Most of my writing has been in praise of the dead, but during the revolutionary period, my creative thoughts turned to portrayals of the living. Then I realized my words could also help those poor black souls still shackled by slavery's firm grip.

My new writing task would delay our marriage a few more months. My ode to Washington came together sooner than I thought it would, so John might not notice my taking time to make poetic remarks about slavery. I felt bound to tell my readers about the evils of slavery. I was not free to write the truth about slavery because I would be punished, perhaps killed, so I had to be subtle and keep the truth hidden in the context of my poetry.

As soon as I finished the poem about Washington, the Boston newspaper printed it. Washington was at his temporary headquarters in Cambridge and read my poem. The newspaper called me a local poet, and so Washington sent one his solders out to find me. The people at the newspaper office knew where I lived. The soldier looking for me carried a sealed letter from Washington.

I sat at my desk putting thoughts against slavery into code words. My words against slavery had to be difficult to find, but obvious for anyone who was looking for them. Deep in thought, the loud, harsh knock on the door startled me back to reality. Opening the door just a little revealed a soldier in uniform with a most resolute expression on his face. He placed a sealed letter from General Washington in my quivering hand.

The letter asked me to visit him and suggested three different times when the visit could take place. He thanked me for writing such an eloquent poem about him, but humbly said he was unworthy of such lavish adulation. Now I know there will be those of you reading this who will say the General could not have had time to visit with me because he was too involved with war preparation. Be certain that the visit took place just as I have written it.

Thinking about which time would be best for me, I caught sight of the uncomfortable look on the face of the soldier. I asked him if he was feeling bad, and he became very uneasy when he realized that his feelings were known to me. Finally, in a stuttering voice, he asked me if he could talk openly with me. I told him to be honest, and made it clear that he should tell the truth and let me handle any difficulties. I thought he was going to say something about having to pick up a poet during such a dangerous time.

After a long pause, the soldier looked into my eyes and said in a faltering voice:

"Ma'am, I ain't educated and have nothing to say about your pretty words. Just know this, my superior hates black people. He would never allow you to see General Washington."

I thanked the soldier for his honesty and then read the sentence from my letter where the General requested an audience with me. The soldier told me that he had heard General Washington say he wanted to meet me.

"Because I know General Washington really wants to meet you," the soldier said, "I'm not going say anything about your being black to my superior."

He told me that when we got to the camp his superior had to admit me. The way it worked was that the wagon was parked a good distance from the office, and the soldier checked in with the superior before letting me enter the General's office. Assuring the soldier that I would never tell anyone how he protected me, finally brought a smile to his face. He said that he felt good "in his heart" and knew that keeping my color unknown to his commanding officer was the right thing to do. The young soldier's uncommon virtue would make possible my visit with General Washington. I thanked him for being so brave and selected nine o'clock on the following

Tuesday morning for my appointment. One could tell that he was comfortable with his decision, but scared, and his fear made talking with him difficult. He had to hear me say, "A soldier cannot be made to do something wrong by his superior" and "No set of rules required him to tell the officer that I was African" before he relaxed just a little. I won him over by letting him read Washington's letter asking to meet me. Much relief came to the soldier's face when he knew he was helping the beloved George Washington.

My soldier friend told me that it was his duty to escort me to the Cambridge headquarters. He asked me to be ready and waiting about 8:15 a.m. as the General was very busy and had stopped making appointments for purely social visits. An exception was being made in my case.

John had already told me that we would have supper at the pub that night. Before he finished knocking, I flung the door open and told him that General Washington wanted to meet me. With almost as much excitement, I told John how I was going to fight slavery with my writing. I shared with him the following words I wrote just after the soldier left:

> But how, presumptuous shall we hope go find
> Divine acceptance with th' almighty mind—
> While yet (O deed Ungengrous!) they disgrace
> And hold in bondage Afric's blameless race?
> Let Virture reign—And thou accord our prayers
> Be victory our's, and generous freedom theirs.

I told John I would use this prayer to end slavery in an elegy or poem. My words would bring comfort to people but also give confidence to those who would like to end the practice of buying and selling people.

I also wanted John to know that I would find a polite way to talk about slavery with General Washington. He knew I was alive with ways to help slaves, because he had been standing in the doorway for several minutes, and I had not brought up our marriage. The main purpose of supper that night was to make marriage plans.

John did not subject me to the embarrassment of asking for more time. Instead, he said,

"I can feel the fire burning in your heart that drives you to help end slavery, and at the moment, it is burning hotter than the flames of our love. I have felt the heat of that love, and I am more than willing to wait until the blaze is rekindled. The evening is yours to talk about whatever you wish. I love you, and I trust that your duties will be but brief interruptions to our lifetime together."

He let me know how impressed he was that General Washington wanted to talk with his future wife. Then he said it would be his privilege to talk with me every day for the rest of his life.

John was too easy with me. I suspected something was wrong, but I did not have time to look into my concern. There is a good chance, however, that John's being so agreeable had something to do with the $1000 I deposited in his bank account. John hated to ask me for money, but he reasoned that we would both benefit from the property deal he was about to close. The $1000 would be repaid from the rent receipts of three Boston stores John was buying. According to John, the property was a very good investment and would pay for itself within 10 years.

I did not sleep well Monday night because I was thinking about what I was going to say to General Washington the next day. Thoughts were racing through my head until the early morning, when sleep finally sealed my eyes for a precious few hours until I got up at sunrise. As I dressed, I rearranged my words and said them aloud so I could hear what they sounded like.

I knew General Washington wanted to talk with me about my ode and not about slavery. I had two goals. My first was to answer his questions about my ode as well as I could. My other goal, perhaps really my main goal, was to prove to him that freedom, by definition, meant not owning people. I had to be very careful not to insult this great man, who was a slaveholder. I meant every word of my ode praising Mr. Washington. I hated that he owned slaves, but I did not want to show that hate in anything I said. More words came to me, and I practiced my speech yet another time. At 8:10 A.M. I was weary of hearing myself and just sat in silence.

Soon my escort was at my front door. A quick look at the mantle clock told me it was exactly 8:15 A.M., and before long I would be talking with General Washington. The officer helped me into the coach and then took a seat across from me. He gave a hand signal, and the driver brought a beautiful pair of horses to full gallop. No words were spoken until we reached the Cambridge road. I could tell that the officer wanted to talk, but he just sat there silently. I thought that his silence was some sort of military procedure. After all, we were at war or nearly at war. I was not sure which.

He apologized in advance, and then said, "Miss Wheatley, I don't think General Washington knows you are a Negro." There was a long pause before he uttered his next sentence. "Miss Wheatley, I don't know how to bring you into the quarters. The slaves must use the back door."

So concerned about what I was going to say, I did not think about Washington not knowing I was a free Negro and the possible complications that might cause. For the poor soldier, those complications played heavily on his mind.

When we got to Washington's Cambridge headquarters, the problem of how I was to enter the building was solved. There was a procedure to follow for all visitors that I think must have been like being arrested. Four friendly people asked me several questions, and I must have given the right answers, because they approved me. They had to protect the Commander in Chief of the Army from both physical and social harm.

After being questioned and thoroughly checked for weapons, I had to state why I wanted to talk with the General. Then I was taken to a cozy room and served refreshments. I was told that the General would see me as soon as he finished installing a new general named Joseph Warren. Joseph Warren, as I recall, was one of the leaders who helped destroy three shipments of British tea just two years ago. Master Wheatley talked about how the men, dressed up like Mohawk Indians, boarded three ships in Boston Harbor right under the British noses. He also said he saw one of the men, and he did not look much like an Indian. Even John Adams, who disliked what he called mob action, said the tea dumping was an act of patriotism.

Thinking about what to say about slavery, so dominated my morning that I'd forgotten to eat breakfast. Not only did the waiting room have the most comfortable chairs I have ever sat in, but right in front of me was a table full of mouthwatering food. The luscious food made me aware of my intense hunger, so I filled a plate and began eating. There was no way to know how long it would take before being called to see the General. The food satisfied my hunger and took my mind off my potential performance in the General's office.

After a few bites of tropical fruit, and while enjoying fresh orange juice, the double doors swung open, hitting the walls with a thunderous sound. My plate nearly went skyward, then I quickly recovered and watched as a phalanx of well-suited men encircled the room. Three of the men walked over to me and started telling me how much Washington appreciated meeting the author who wrote so well. I had the idea that besides being kind to me, they were also trying to understand why Washington would give me an appointment. Out of the corner of my eye, I could see five or six men seemingly inspecting the room. The last members of the group took guard positions at the corners, and two stood on each side of the entrance. Without being asked, a servant came forward and took my plate.

The men talking with me were so kind and attractive that I gave them all of my attention. The other soldiers kept moving about the room and then stopped one by one until they surrounded the area. Being a tailor, I could not help but appreciate their fine uniforms. A strange hush settled over the room when the double doors opened again, and the General entered. He was in an impressive gray-blue dress uniform, but not the least bit showy. He seemed larger than anyone in the room. He was a big man, but you were also drawn to him as if he had some special power.

He came right to our group, and I could see that he was startled to see a tiny black woman talking with his information officers. He said nothing for a few seconds, and then uttered a simple, "Miss Wheatley, what a pleasure to meet you," with a high voice not equal to his mighty appearance. His facial expression told me that he had not been told that I was a Negro. I thanked him for the honor of meeting him and told him I knew how difficult it was to make the meeting possible. He invited me into his office, and his voice returned to a more normal pitch. A secretary came into the room with us and wrote down every word said. The secretary was also an armed soldier, so there was a military reason for his being there.

I felt very relaxed in Washington's presence. He ordered us a pot of the most wonderful tea I had ever drunk, and we began to talk. In short order, he knew everything about me there was to know. Then he asked what caused me to write the ode about him.

As I told him the road-building story, his face formed a warm grin. After I finished, he told me why he was smiling. He said that our soldiers were able to get ready for war with the British all around us. They did not have the money for uniforms so they dressed in regular clothes so that as they got ready for war, they looked like ordinary people working on the road.

The British marched around in spotless, red uniforms, while all around them were ragged colonists doing what looked like hard labor. They saw just a few in uniform. With hardly any men to defend the colonies, the British must have felt they could easily defeat us. Washington told me that the British were totally unprepared to face the actual strength of the colonial army.

Before I could bring up the subject of slavery, General Washington told me he planned to free his slaves upon his death. I told him that I had gotten my freedom upon the death of my Mistress because my Master followed his dying wife's wishes. I also told General Washington that Mrs. Wheatley established a bank account for me upon her death. The General almost apologetically told me that his wife, Martha, had not made the same provisions (freedom upon her death) for her slaves. Her slaves would remain slaves even after she died. He said his intentions were to get her to change her mind on this issue.

I was putting together my remarks on freedom in my mind when a loud knock startled me. The General barked the word "Enter," and a soldier stepped smartly into the room. There was an exchange of salutes. The soldier seemed to stare right past the General as he said,

"General Washington, sir, you have a working lunch today with the division commanders."

The soldier stopped talking and just stood there for a few seconds. Then he said, "General Warren will be there, sir."

General Washington thanked the soldier and told him they would leave for the meeting in fifteen minutes. General Washington thanked me for coming and told me how much he enjoyed talking with me. Even though he had a very important meeting, he walked me out of the building to my awaiting coach. He even helped me into the coach and then told me he was going to create a trust fund for his slaves so that after his death they would be solvent financially. He thanked me for giving him the idea.

I shall never forget my meeting with General Washington, a great man and a true gentleman. I am sorry that we did not talk much about freedom and equality. I hope that what I did get to say to the general might in time cause him to help the many Africans in America. I tried to get him to understand that we were brought here against our wills, and that the colonies would never be the land of the free as long as slavery was allowed to continue. I could tell that Washington was moved by what I said, but that he still supported slavery. Also, his military concerns did not allow us enough time for a thoughtful talk. I had done my best and the meeting was over. I rode home silently, heavy-hearted with the thought that our new America would not be the home of the free.

I enjoyed the memories of my talk with General Washington for weeks after the meeting, but I was bothered by the fact that we had spent so little time talking about the evils of slavery. Also, the time went so fast that I felt good about even getting to say a few things about freedom for slaves. Given his busy schedule, and me being an African, I should be happy just to have gotten to talk with General Washington.

The General was so courteous that it was not easy for me to tell if the few words I said against slavery troubled him. He listened to what I had to say and directed all his attention toward me. He often nodded his head in agreement, and his reassuring appearance convinced me that I had said enough about the matter.

I felt guilty for not taking a more active role in the abolitionist movement. To soothe my conscience, and with newfound courage, I began to hide antislavery thoughts in my poems. I had to be guarded about what I wrote, because I did not want to be labeled a troublemaker. It was difficult enough for me to sell my writing, but no colonist would buy books from me if they thought I was plotting against slavery. If I was found out, I could have been punished, or even hanged. I no longer had the protection of the Wheatley family.

I was so good at concealing antislavery ideas in my poetry that I sometimes found them hard to find myself. If anyone did discover them, they were so vague I could argue that I did not mean them to be against slavery. I took comfort in the thought that readers some day would find my hidden antislavery words. As I wrote, I thought about the expressions on the faces of people keen on understanding my poetry as they figured out my code words. My efforts to end slavery were minor compared to those of others who risked their lives trying to stop slavery in our time.

Slaves tricked slave owners and slave catchers by communicating escape routes using common everyday things like songs and quilts. Songs were one of our best ways of giving directions to slaves on the run. Slave owners enjoyed listening to slaves singing at night after we had finished our work. They had no idea we were telling runaways to follow the North Star to New York. I could not believe that even so obvious a pointer as "The Drinking Gourd Song" went unnoticed.

I worry about telling you how we helped each other, because this book could get into the wrong hands and be used against us, but I must divulge one more messaging method, because it is so brilliant. Some day, the world must know that slaves were smart, but we had to play dumb in order to survive. Slaves who acted smart were often killed immediately, and that extinguished any hope one had to learn. Slave owners allowed slaves to make quilts as long as every third quilt was given to their owners. Colonists loved our quilts, and many asked us to teach them how we made them.

The big house slaves regularly aired the master's bedding, so these quilts provided perfect posters for escape routes as they hung from clotheslines and fences. I can describe one route that will close when I finish this book. Routes were opened and shut frequently to protect slaves on the run.

What looked like big flowers on a quilt were actually paths through New York into Canada. Flower quilts also told slaves how much time it took to get to safe stops and the distance to freedom houses. The petal of the flower in the upper right-hand corner was a map showing the trail from Ithaca to Farmer, New York. I give you this much information so you have some idea of the details our quilts provided. Again, this book could get into the wrong hands, so I will disclose no more except to say you would be amazed at all the detail we can put into what looks like a regular quilt design.

Some slave owners did not know how cruel their overseers could be. Owners did not deal directly with slaves, but hired overseers to do so and gave them total control. The evil of some slave owners and overseers caused me to suggest poetically that like Cain, they were marked with "a diabolic die."

Allow me to quote the poem "On Being brought from AFRICA to AMERICA" as an example of my encoding:

Twas mercy brought me from my Pagan land,
Taught my benighted soul to understand
That there's a God, that there's a Saviour too:
Once I redemption neither sought nor knew.
Some view our sable race with scornful eye,
Their colour is a diabolic die.
Remember, Christians, Negroes, black as Cain,
May be refin'd, and join th' angelic train.

One reason I could encode antislavery messages in my poetry was that no one expected a slave to be capable of such a task. My writing appeared to approve of bigotry, but actually, I condemned it. In the poem just cited, I appear to say that my creator's mercy allowed for my leaving Africa, but slaves knew my words meant that we did not ask to come to America, but were brought against our will, and that my brown skin would fly to heaven as well as their white skin.

In another poem, I used beautiful words to secretly tell white people that the same Lord who died for them had redeemed slaves. In my poems, I write about a God who equally loves everyone, including slaves. Once you know the code you will see that my poetry condemned slavery. Illiterate slaves knew the words I used to put down slavery. Slaves used a system that gave different meanings for common words. I won't tell you the system, but I will give you a simple example. If I say that my Master is good to another slave, I am really saying the Master is bad. The Master thinks he is getting praise, but the slave knows the truth. Outwitting slaveholders was not a difficult task.

When I went to London, I noticed the difference between the English and the colonists. The working class in England was polished and articulate. In the colonies, it was not unusual to hear crude words and see poor manners even in the homes of rich families. I found myself wanting to side with the loyalists and move to England.

Of course, I was influenced by how I was treated on my brief stay in London. I am a free person, and I could live anywhere in the world, including Africa. My years in Boston and the many friends I have made, especially John, endear me to this place. I want to help make the colonies a better place to live by listing our faults and praising our strengths in my poetry.

I trick people with words in my poetry. The encoded words in the passage just quoted a few pages back were "die," "refin'd," "sable," and "Cain." Go back and read the passage again to see if you can find my hidden messages. I will tell you that my words showed the slaveholder's bigotry and the sham of white self-importance. My poetry, like many things in this world, is not what it seems.

A close look at my poetry will show that I condemned false abolitionists who helped slavers by using the blue dye and sugar products. The slavers would exchange slaves and colonial rum in the islands off the coast of Africa and the West Indies for things wanted by the colonists. False abolitionists did not buy people, but buying the other things kept the slave trade going. Without a market for the West Indies' products, the slave trade ends.

Some day my code will be known to everyone. Then people who read my poetry will see how much I hated slavery and how I supported those who tried to end it. I take great pleasure in thinking that my words might cause a change in the corrupt logic and ethics that permitted the owning of humans.

The name "abolitionists" was given to people who wanted to free the slaves and end slavery. Mr. Wheatley had some Quaker friends in Rhode Island who freed every slave they owned. Hearing white abolitionists speak out against slavery encouraged me to work diligently to help their cause.

Because I was treated as special by the Wheatleys, I had a much easier life than did most slaves. I also regret that I was the only Wheatley slave given freedom. I was in the Wheatley home when the other slaves were planning an escape. The plan was to go aboard a British ship just before it set sail to England. As of the time I write this book, they have not made their escape.

Fear of being caught, at first, kept me from putting antislavery code words in my writing, but gradually I got the courage to continue my poetic protest. I think I got very good at using double meanings in my poems that asked for an end to slavery. I know I will not live to know the results of my protest writing. I will say more about my bad feelings toward slavery in the next chapter. I pray the antislavery thoughts I put in my poems, once read, will enter the hardest heart and soften the harsh feelings some hold for Africans.

Imagination!
Who can sing thy force?
Or who describe the swiftness of thy course?

Phillis Wheatley

Chapter 11–Becoming a Mother

Before I write this chapter, I want to apologize for my awkward prose. I thought prose would be easier to write than poetry. I was wrong. Writing prose and poetry are both difficult. I sometimes think about machines that could record our words, saving us from the work of writing. While I was in England, I recall reading a description of a mechanical writing machine invented by a man named Henry Mill.

These thoughts about things that would make writing easier digress from my task of telling you about myself. I must do what I do best, and that is inventing with words, rather than tools and machines, if I expect to complete this book anytime soon. However, I thought you might like to know a little bit about my fanciful brain.

I wonder if everyone has to do as much rewriting as I have done on this book. Perhaps it will be of comfort to young people to know that, in order to write a simple sentence correctly, they should be prepared to rewrite it several times. Seldom does the perfect sentence happen on first try. There is always some fixing to do. You will find mistakes in my writing. Truly, none of us are exempt from mistakes, so do not let fears of making a mistake keep you from doing what you want to do.

I was not ill-used by my Master or any member of his household, and I had only one Master during my entire servitude. Young Nat, I think, had intentions toward me, but that could be attributed to being alone together in England. Both Nat and I knew a physical relationship was wrong, and we simply did what was right.

I am happy that at this point, you know about half of my story. I am also troubled that a reader might think of me as being vain because of my good fortune. Had I not had access to a large supply of scrap paper, this book would never have been written.

Times are very difficult for John and me. Our finances failed, and bad health overtook both of us. I must get finished with my story, so I can use precious time to write poetry and do household chores.

As I said before, it bothers me to write about myself. In order to write this peek at slavery, I had to remind myself I was giving those who read my book a true depiction of slavery. I did my best not to mislead anyone as regards the life of this slave. The reader must trust me, but at least you know this is a first-hand account and not a story embellished from multiple retellings.

At last, I can tell you about the main reason I did not go to England or return to Africa. I stayed in Boston to marry John Peters. I found myself sitting on the porch of the Wheatley home. Nathaniel inherited the house and offered me a place to stay as I prepared for marriage.

I recall that the war with Great Britain started almost in the Wheatley front yard. Just a few years earlier, from the steps of the house, I saw my dear friend, Tuck, mortally wounded. Tuck was not supposed to be with the minutemen when he got shot. He was having an argument with a Mr. Heath, and the British soldiers mistook the loud arguing for a battle charge. They fired a round, and Tuck lay dead. I thought about Tuck's tenacity as I started making plans for my wedding.

It is now difficult for me to write. I am very tired, although I have had enough sleep. I fear the illness that I had on my arrival in Boston has returned. I have some of the same conditions, but I dare not tell John. Most of my days are good, so perhaps it will go away. Because all but a few doctors are involved in the war, it is very difficult to get medical help. The ones left are very old and demand cash before seeing you. John is struggling to eke out a living, and I do not want to burden him with more problems.

John and I were married in the Methodist church on April 15, 1778. Obour Tanner was my Maid of Honor. Nathaniel Wheatley gave me to John, and Mary served as one of my maids. I never thought this would happen, but the *Boston Evening Post* filled one page with a description of our wedding. This was an unheard of privilege we were granted. Anyone who reads the story about our wedding will be transported to the church that day. Being overwhelmed by joy kept me from noticing that separate seating by race was not used at our wedding. The newspaper wrote that the ushers seated guests as if everyone were of one race. The article said that none of the guests seemed bothered by the equal treatment at the wedding and the reception that followed. That feeling of equality was my best wedding gift, after I read the newspaper account. I hope my wedding was a glimpse of what the future holds for America.

John and I departed in a shower of rice. Sadly, as I looked back, I saw my friends returning to the roles of slave and master. That beautiful present of equality was snatched away by reality.

I procrastinated on my work and enjoyed being pampered by John. We were truly a matched pair. John was educated, as was I. Both of us were ambitious, free, and able to get along with all people, and both of us wanted children. It was not long until I was pregnant with our first child.

The child carried well until about the seventh month. Then I knew something was wrong, but said nothing to John. It was not possible for poor former slaves to see a doctor. Just being poor usually kept you from going to a doctor, but if you were both poor and a former slave, then there was no way you would ever get a doctor's help.

What I said in the last paragraph is true, but I want you to know that a few doctors would sometimes treat the poor and Africans. These doctors seemed to worry most about the health of children and mothers, but there were so few doctors in Boston that clinics, even for those able to pay for services, opened only a few hours on Wednesday.

I managed to make it to my ninth month with my pregnancy. I tried as best I could to locate my old friend Obour, who had a wealth of medical knowledge. Obour was bought by an American physician who allowed her to be part of his clinic. She was very smart and knew medicine as well as many doctors. It was impossible for me to travel, and I never could get a message to Obour. John knew I was having troubles and managed to be at home almost the entire last month. He told me he was doing paperwork. I appreciated his concern, but I also knew we lost a month's wages as a result of his constant care. Finally, my time arrived, and John ran six blocks to fetch the midwife.

John told me how much he loved me, and then left the room. The midwife examined me, and I recall a pained look on her face. She told me quietly, almost in a whisper, that my baby was not presenting properly. She said I needed a doctor, but then realized that was impossible.

In desperation, the midwife adjusted the baby and cut me enough to allow passage into the world. The mid-wife apologized for the pain she caused. I told her truthfully that I felt no pain. She laid my baby on my shrunken abdomen, and he expired with a tiny whimper. I didn't even get to suckle him.

The midwife began remorseful crying. She explained that a doctor could have moved the child properly without damaging the baby's delicate head and neck. Somehow, I was composed enough to tell her that she saved my life and could take no blame for the death of our little boy. She continued to cry, saying,

"I don't have the proper instruments or training. I killed a little baby." We could not get her to stop.

The sight of my worsening condition must have brought the midwife to her senses, and she turned her attention to me again. I vaguely remember her pushing on my stomach. I was so weak that I could not move. I felt like I was drifting away, and then I must have passed out. I did not awaken until early the next morning.

When I awakened, my first sight was the midwife sitting beside the bed holding my hand, and then John came into focus. When our eyes met, he burst into tears and simultaneously wailed the words,

"I'm so sorry, my love. I'm so, so sorry."

We lost our first child. Grief overtook me, and I languished for days, unable to function. I made a living writing eulogies and was in great demand. I was respected and admired for bringing comfort to a bereaved family with my quill and ink. Yet, I could do nothing to bring relief to myself. Nor was I positively affected by the words of friends. Even worse than the grief was the horrible thought deep inside that I would never be a mother.

I kept my thoughts to myself so as not to hurt John. All the abuse I suffered as a slave took its toll, causing me to be quite frail, but John and I had each other. I am unable to fully express the relief I gained from our marriage bond, except to say that love heals everything.

Because of the war with Great Britain, I lost all my well-paying English publishing contacts. John and I were unable to find employment in Boston. Our meager bank account was quickly gone, and we lost all of our property. We had to move to a squatters' village outside of Boston, where we took refuge in an abandoned hay shed.

Under these conditions, I bore a second child. This young man, Alex Peters, is an exact replica of his proud father. I was so relieved when the same midwife who helped with my first son delivered a robust Alexander. As I nursed him, I wrote these words, "Almighty, in these wond'rous works of thine, What Pow'r, What Wisdom, and Goodness shine!" Oh, how I love motherhood!

John and I became victims of our black skin. We could not gain freedom from an evil worse than slavery—racism. Had we been white, John would have been a successful lawyer and I a favored writer. We will not know true liberation until we cross the river of life. The Lord, no doubt, will allow us to partake of that same reward He bestowed on Lazarus.

John could find no source of income and had to resort to selling liquor to the lowly inhabitants of our village. What little money they had was spent on alcohol to numb the pain of poverty and hatred. My husband had to bear the guilt from earning money as the purveyor of sin and shame.

In spite of all our problems, I never stopped writing. I completed two books of poetry in hopes of finding a publisher and a way out of our dire circumstances. I should also tell you that poverty kept us from having another child.

John tried in vain to find someone to publish my work. I could not go with him because of my condition. He had to sell more and more liquor because his supplier decreased his commission. We are now totally at the mercy of that vile, unethical man.

John brought me a most difficult request. A gentleman from Philadelphia had contacted him and offered to buy my books outright, with no royalties coming to us. He offered John enough money for us to survive for about a month. I had worked three years on those books. I had to decide to trade all of that time and labor for fifty dollars.

I decided to do it, but found almost unbearable the thought that my work would be credited to another person upon publication. I could not allow my ego to intervene in John's efforts to support his family, so I gave my consent, and John left the next morning to make the sale.

We decided to use all the money from the sale of my books to move back into Boston. We found a boarding house with a small apartment out back for rent. It was not too far from the little cottage I first rented on my release from slavery. John found work with the *Boston Chronicle* as a pressman. He laughed when he came home from work covered with ink. He said it was an ideal job for a man of his color. The wages were just barely enough to pay our rent.

The second day on the job, John forgot to take his lunch bucket. I bundled up Alex, and we delivered the bucket to John. He could not leave his position on the press, so I gave it to a man in the office. He stared at me and then said, "Aren't you Louisa Wheatley?"

I answered that I was, but now I am married to John Peters. He asked me if I still wrote poetry, and I told him I had been too busy taking care of my family to write.

As I started to walk away, he asked me if I had time to talk with him about a way I could make money and take care of our son at the same time. We went into a small room that was stacked from floor to ceiling with type and parts to the big presses. He cleared a chair for Alex and me and then showed me a page that had a blank space along the edge. He told me that the blank spaces caused a typesetting problem that could easily be fixed by a poem the same size as the space.

He told me that if I would write several poems of different lengths to fill those spaces, he would pay me the equivalent of two hours of typesetting for each poem. He said that would be very helpful to the newspaper and give me a small income. He told me that he knew my work and had no concern about the quality of my writing. He also said that once a week they would print a full-length poem, if I were able to accomplish that task.

I thanked the gentleman for the job and went home feeling very happy that I would once again get paid for writing poetry, taking some of the pressure from John. I knew I could get most of my writing done while Alex slept. We now had a nicer apartment in Boston, thanks to John's labor, and my income would be just enough for food and expenses. I have all but forgotten our first home that the sale of my book allowed us to rent.

We are poor, but very rich. John's love fulfilled all my earthly needs, and I know God's love will bring my desired haven. Please know now that I am at peace, in spite of our circumstances. I pray that you share that same peace.

*Can Afric's Muse forgetful prove
Or can such Friendship! Laurel-crown'd,
To smiling Graces all surround
With ev'ry heav'nly Art*

*Phillis Wheatley
Boston, December 12, 1773*

Chapter 12—A Friend in Braintree

Shortly after we moved into our new apartment, I got a message from John Adams inviting me to his home. He had heard about my visit with General Washington and wanted me to know firsthand how concerned he was that the commander in chief of the army kept slaves. He wrote that he thought it not possible for someone to be fighting for the Glorious Cause while at the same time enslaving people. He also wondered how a man with such wealth could understand the needs of people with more modest means.

Mr. Adams lived some distance south of our home. He did not mention Alex in the invitation, so I assumed that I was to come alone. He wrote in his letter that the demands of his law practice and small farm along with his Continental Congress work did not allow him to visit me. He also reminded me that he had defended the redcoats who had killed my friend Tuck in the Boston Massacre and told me that he understood if I chose not to make the trip. However, he assured me that the road to his home was well-traveled and safe, especially since the fighting was about finished. If I came the next weekend, I could ride with his wife, Abby, who would be in Boston on Friday.

He told me that Mrs. Adams would be with her friend Mercy Warren as she, Mrs. Warren, visits a publisher in Boston. He tried to entice me with a description of the big, comfortable coach of the Warrens. I found out that Abby loved to make these trips with Mercy and talk about Shakespeare, Milton, and other great writers. They also spent the time talking about the patriotic plays Mrs. Warren wrote. Nobody knew they were her plays because she did not use her real name. Mr. Adams wrote that Abby would especially enjoy being with two accomplished writers. Mrs. Adams would tell me that she regretted not having any schooling, but, like me, she did a good job of self-education. Mr. Adams would take me home, since he had work to do in Boston on Monday.

I had wanted to meet Mr. John Adams for a long time and hoped I could take advantage of his kind offer. I knew Sam Adams, John's cousin, but I had been told that John was nothing like Sam. There was a problem. I could not leave Alex, and we had just moved into the neighborhood, so I did not know anyone well. I knew John would do anything to make me happy, so I had to refuse the offer without telling him about it. While I was penning the message telling Mr. Adams that I could not come, another message arrived from him. The first line of that message asked me to forgive him for not taking into account my son in the original invitation.

Mr. Adams wrote that he had a son a little older than Alex, and the two of them could play together while we visited. It would be a special treat for his son to have a house guest that weekend. This would be an especially good weekend to visit because the church had a special program planned for the children. There would be an entire afternoon of games followed by a puppet show that would play here before going on to Philadelphia. He also wrote that John was welcome, as they had plenty of room. He again said he was sorry for not including my family in his first message. He said Abby had told him to be sure to invite us, but that in his haste he left out those important words.

"Fortunately," he joked, "I am not as forgetful in my legal writing as I am in my social writing. I am again sorry, and I hope my forgetfulness has not troubled you, because I meant no disrespect."

When John came home that night, we talked about the invitation. My reply had to be on the stage the next morning to get to Mr. Adams on time. Without pause, John said that Alex and I should accept the invitation, but that he could not come because of his work. He told me that he knew about John Adams because he had just set the type for a story about Adams. According to John, Mr. Adams, better than anyone, made it clear that the colonies were about to win a historical war. My wonderful husband let me know that to have his wife welcomed by both General Washington and John Adams was an honor for both him and our son. My letter of acceptance was on the stage the next morning.

When I told Alex about the trip, he got very excited. He loved to go to the country. Usually, that meant a short trip to the outskirts of Boston and the purchase of fresh farm products. We had never stayed overnight in the country. Also, Alex had never been with a friend for three days in a row. I was not much help because the closest thing to a country home for me had been the visits to Dr. Craig, but Dr. Craig's home was so close to town that you did not feel like you were in the country. Also, I spent all my time there doing the same things as I did in the Wheatley home. Both of us would experience the real country for the first time.

I packed two cases, with our Sunday clothes taking up most of the second case. I wrote a personal note to the Adamses on the inside cover of my book of poems and then wrapped it in some beautiful paper I saved for just such an occasion. Alex spent the week making John Adams a board game he liked to play. Using a piece of wood from an old crate, he rubbed it smooth with sandstone. His dad brought home some ink, and Alex lined the board. Finally, he found eighteen small, polished stones to use for game pieces. Nine of the stones were dark and the other nine light. Alex learned the game on visits to his father's work. Some men who came to America from Spain played the game on every break and taught the game to Alex.

Alex had made a game board for himself and often played with his father on Sundays. He was very proud of the new board, the gift for John Quincy Adams, because he fixed mistakes he had made on the first one. Mr. Adams named his son John with the middle name of Quincy. The son was called John Q. to distinguish him from his father. Neither John nor I asked Alex to make the gift. He did it on his own. I cautioned him not to expect a gift in return. I told him that being able to stay three days in the country was our present.

Alex is amazing. He is only five years old and already reading. He read all the way to Braintree while Mrs. Adams, Mrs. Warren and I talked about everything from politics to how much we miss our husbands. Abby and I had husbands whose work kept them away from home. Poor Mrs. Warren lost her husband in one of the early battles on Breed's Hill. She now spends her time writing plays and republican papers. Alex did not stop reading during the entire trip.

About halfway there, we stopped at a delightful tavern for a light lunch. Mrs. Adams insisted on paying for Alex and me. Embarrassingly, the tavern owner came over to our table and asked me if I was the Louisa that recited poetry in Boston about five years ago. I told him I was indeed that Louisa, and he told me how much he enjoyed my poems. In fact, he had a framed copy of my poem "On Friendship" hanging in his office. I stopped him and told him that there were much more important women than me sitting at the table. I then introduced Mrs. Adams and Mrs. Warren.

Alex just sat there taking in all of this. He had not seen his mother treated so royally before. As I think about it, Alex was familiar with the struggles of his mother and father. The owner would not allow us to pay for our meals. He brought his framed copy of "On Friendship" to our table and politely asked me to sign it. I not only signed the poem, but asked him if he would allow me to recite it for him and the other patrons. Indeed, he said it would be a great honor and a momentous event for his tavern to have Louisa Wheatley (he did not know that I was married) recite a poem here.

He apologized for not having a stage, but engaged some steps that allowed me to get on the bar. Before I began the poem, I gave a little talk on friendship and told everyone that today I made three new friends. I told them that I was on my way to visit yet another friend and great American, Mr. John Adams, and then from memory I said:

"Let amicitia in her ample reign
Extend her notes to a Celestial strain
Benevolent far more divinely Bright
Amor like me doth triumph at the sight
When my thoughts in gratitude imploy
Mental Imaginations give me joy
Now let my thoughts in Contemplation steer
The Footsteps of the Superlative fair."

When I finished, I bowed to the audience, and the tavern owner helped me off the makeshift stage. The clapping did not stop until I stood up again. I thanked everyone and said I would do nothing else to keep them from eating the delicious food.

The food was very good. Because this was the only stop between Boston and Braintree, the owner could have served anything to the travelers, but what he served was as good as some of the best food I had eaten in Boston. Alex asked me the name of the man who had been so nice to us, and I realized that I had not gotten his name. I thanked Alex for asking me the question, because not to get his name would have been very rude.

The gentleman gave us privacy as we enjoyed his food, but after we had eaten, I went over to him and apologized for not asking his name. He then apologized to me for being so forward. I assured him that I appreciated everything he had said and told him how much it meant to me for Alex to have been there and heard all those good things said about his mother. He said his name was Captain Eliphelet Newell. He told me he was a friend of both Sam and John Adams and that he would appreciate it if I would give Mr. John Adams his greetings.

With the meal finished, and Captain Newell not accepting payment, we all thanked him and left his place with the promise to return soon. Our carriage drivers helped us board, and then they climbed on the coachman's bench while the lackeys took their places on the rear of the coach. With a sharp command and a snap of the reins, the carriage was once again rolling toward Braintree.

Forgetting Mr. Adams' message, I told Mrs. Adams that sitting in her carriage was just like being in a fancy Boston parlor. She told me that the carriage belonged to

Mrs. Warren. Mrs. Warren then thanked me and said the carriage was one of the last things Dr. Warren bought before his untimely death.

"He wanted me to travel in comfort and paid 120 Pounds Sterling for the carriage right before the tea incident in Boston. I remember how concerned he was that the English carriage company would not make delivery."

She told me that she seldom traveled to Boston without stopping for Abby, because it takes four horses, two coachmen, and two lackeys to operate the carriage. Mr. Adams graciously allows his coachman and lackey to join with mine on trips to Boston. Mrs. Adams told me that Alex and I would make the trip back to Boston in their carriage, which is nice, but not nearly as comfortable as the Warrens' coach.

The Adams' home was right beside the road. I would have thought that it would have been down a long tree-lined lane, but there it stood, no more than thirty feet from the road. It was a large home standing very near a similar, but smaller, house to its north. Mr. Adams told me later that the small house next to his present home was his birthplace. He said that he paid for his Harvard education by selling much of the land he inherited. His children would inherit this place, and then he and Abby would move to a new home not too far down the road. He assured me that the new home would have a separate, large library and an English garden. He said this because we both shared a love for books and nature.

Mrs. Warren left almost immediately for her home in Plymouth. Although her carriage had a lantern on each corner, she did not like to travel after dark. Mr. Adams told me how pleased he was that I agreed to visit his family. Alex and John Quincy, the Adams' son, made instant friends, even though Alex was much younger than the Adams lad. Although the home was of simple construction, it was large, having been extended at least twice, as I could tell. The single front door was oversized and had some attractive carving on it. Mr. Adams swung the door open and told the lackeys to put my case in the downstairs guest bedroom and for Alex to make himself at home in John Quincy's room upstairs. He told us that after we freshened up, we could sit outside and visit until supper.

The Adams family did not keep slaves. All of the help were paid a fair wage, and most had been with the Adams family for many years. We sat outside on a nice lawn talking as the smoke from the chimney wafted the delightful smell of baking bread and pot roast in the air. Mr. Adams, I think unknowingly, was questioning me much like he would a witness in court. Abby put a stop to this tactic with a rather stern rebuke. She told John that this wasn't a courtroom inquest, and that his guests had traveled a good distance to enjoy his company, not his courtroom behavior.

I felt unnerved and thought John was going to give Abby a tart reply. I had not been there more than twenty minutes, and I was going to be caught right in the middle of a fight between two people I barely knew. Instead, he thanked her for telling him that he was distressing me. Then he looked at me and said,

"I ask your forgiveness. I am fearful that my hard questioning hurt our relationship. I assure you that it was only the pressure of my limited time that led to my lack of thought for your comfort. Please accept this, my second apology. From this point forward, I promise you that I will show concern for your comfort and control my curiosity."

I stood there dumbfounded. Here was Washington's equal, yet he bore Mrs. Adam's corrections as if he were a servant. Now mind you, he was not nearly as informal as Mr. Franklin, but by now, I knew that when it came to Mr. Franklin, there were no comparisons. I met Washington at his headquarters during the war, and I was visiting Adams near the end of the war at his home. Perhaps if I had visited Washington in his home, he would have seemed more normal instead of godlike, but then how would George and Martha Washington have handled having a former slave in their home? These thoughts circled in my head, and then the entire room began to circle. I felt my knees give way and I crumpled in a heap on the floor.

I awoke in Abigail Amelia's downstairs bedroom. She was the delight of the Adams family and had a well-furnished bedroom complete with a small library in one corner. As my senses came to me, I was able to focus on the books and recall when I had read each one. I felt a breeze and turned to see a smiling Mrs. Adams fanning me. I wanted to get up, but I still felt a bit shaky. Then I heard Alex saying over and over,

"Momma, I love you."

John suggested that all but Mrs. Adams leave the room and give me time to recuperate. He asked John Quincy to show Alex the new pony and the other animals, but to be back in about an hour for supper. Without another word spoken, everyone except Mrs. Adams quietly left the room. I felt better as soon as I heard Alex's glee when he spotted the little pony in the pasture just behind the house. I could see him through the window as he ran, pulling John Quincy, who was trying to hold Alex's hand.

Mrs. Adams said aloud, "Your Alex is a smart, precious little boy."

I quickly said, "Thank you, ma'am", and then sat up on the edge of the bed. The bed was very high, and I was still unstable, so I could not stand up without help. I just sat there for a few minutes, and then asked Mrs. Adams if she would support me as I got to my feet. I told her that I was very thirsty and that I felt like I needed to walk around. She offered to bring me a glass of water, but I said that, with her help, I thought I could make it to the kitchen. One of the nicest things about the Adams' home was that it had a pump in the kitchen.

Now that is enough about my embarrassing fainting spell. I started not to put it in the book, except that it showed how kind and gentle the Adams were. They put me in their best bed and did not leave my side until I recovered. They offered to get a doctor, but I would have none of that. I told them that I was very frightened, having never before visited the home of such important people. That statement brought a laugh from both John and Abigail. They said that they were just ordinary people, and they were worried about entertaining such a well-known poet and writer. That statement made me laugh aloud.

Through the kitchen window, I could see Alex atop the little pony riding alongside John Quincy on his steed. I asked if we could go outside and watch the children until the meal was ready, and John said, "Follow me." He led us to a bench under a small tree large enough for the three of us. As I watched Alex galloping around the property with his friend John Quincy, I asked Mr. Adams about the tree-covered hill in the distance. An attractive rock wall outlined the land on which the homes sat. The two sturdy Adams homes seemed planted in a meadow that extended all the way to a distant mountain.

Mr. Adams told me that at one time, all of the land within eyesight was Adams property. He inherited the land, but had to sell much of it in order to pay for his Harvard law degree. During the past few years, he had bought back much of the original land and some attractive new land just a few miles north of the home site. Then he confided that they were land rich, but did not have much cash on deposit. He figured they would have to sell land again to pay for the college education of John Quincy. Just then, a bell pealed several times, and Mr. Adams said it was supper time. The children heard the same bell and galloped toward the barn.

There would be eight of us at the main table, and the cooks ate at a table in the kitchen. The six Adams children all had specified chores to do, serving the food and cleaning up after the meal. They insisted that neither Alex nor I do any of the chores. On the wall in the dining room hung a picture of Susanna Adams, who died at the young age of two. I did not know until I saw the picture that they had lost a child. I told Mrs. Adams that we lost our first child at birth and how hard that had been on John and me. All she could say was,

"Yes, I know."

A moment of silence followed as we shared our pain while looking deep into each other's eyes. Mr. Adams put his arms around both of us and led us into the parlor.

I sat down and could see that Alex had managed to become part of the cleanup crew after all. I knew there was no way he would sit back and watch his friends work while he did nothing. In that regard, he was just like his father. Soon, a delightful chorus of children's voices came from the kitchen as the children sang together while they worked. The cooks all lived in nice houses not too far from the main house. They came in to visit, but quickly bid us goodbye as they went home to be with their own families.

Mr. Adams told me that all his help lived on the property. I asked him about the stone fence that surrounded the place. He said it was built with rocks from the field and that he had helped build the part running parallel with the road when he was just a little older than Alex. He said that his family had never owned slaves, and that all of the work was done by family or hired help. The help was treated so well that a new generation was continuing the work begun by their grandparents.

Then he told me that his three sons and he were working on a new wall on property not far from there. Eventually, a home would be built on the land outlined by the wall for the oldest male. They would do the same thing for the middle son. The elder Adams and his wife would move to a beautiful property not more than a mile away, leaving the original home for the youngest male. He added that he thought his daughters would marry and live with their husbands somewhere else, just as Abby came to live with him. However, he said they would also be welcome if they wanted to live on the Adams' property.

The children had finished all the chores and were playing a game outside. Their laughter filled the room, but I had not noticed. I was listening so closely to Mr. and Mrs. Adams that I was unmindful of my surroundings. I told them much of what you are reading in this book. They made me feel so relaxed and at home that I dominated the next few hours with our family history. When the clock chimed nine times, Mrs. Adams said that we would all gather for prayers with the children before they went to bed. Tears formed in my eyes as I heard Alex say,

"Thank you, Lord, for my new friends and for allowing me to spend the weekend in the country."

I was so proud of my little five-year-old son. I thought to myself that, the Lord willing, and with the help of men like John Adams, slavery would end, and Alex would always be free.

The children were tired, and sleep quickly hushed their tiny voices. As we sat listening to sleep quiet the children, I told the Adams about the magical character the children of my village thought flew around and sealed our eyes. We knew it was true because the remnants of its work were found in our eyes when we awoke. They enjoyed my story and wanted to hear more about Africa. At Mr. Adams' suggestion, we moved to the large room on the road side of the house so we would not disturb the children. The room was a parlor, but one corner also served as his law office. Law books filled several shelves. We sat in the front portion of the room on overstuffed furniture. The glow of the lanterns made the room even cozier. We agreed that when the clock struck ten it would be time for the adults to go to bed because Sunday was going to be a busy day.

I could not help but notice that the parlor floor boards were very wide. Mr. Adams saw me staring at the planks and said the floor was made from the king's lumber. When his father lived here, he had to give his best timber to King George as a form of tax.

"As an act of rebellion, my father made this floor from the tree that was supposed to go to the king. So you see, my father was a revolutionary long before we started this war. His was a revolution of the mind and heart, but it gave me the courage to be a leader in the separation from England. Now, I must stop talking and start listening, or else all of our efforts for this weekend could be for naught." Abby quickly agreed with what he said.

They patiently allowed me to talk about Africa even after ten chimes sounded. It occurred to me that Africa had been the center of the conversation ever since we put the children to bed. I apologized for talking so much. Abigail laughed, and said, "I promise you, John would have broken in the second his interest waned, so he must have enjoyed what you had to say. I know I did. Speaking for the both of us, we have never heard such interesting things about your country. You have educated us, and we thank you."

Mr. Adams spoke next and told me that I made firm his already strong anti-slavery beliefs.

"Before we go to bed, however, I would appreciate knowing how you could write such a beautiful ode about General Washington, since he was a slaveholder."

I had been talking most of the night and it would soon be eleven. I told him that I would be much more detailed tomorrow, but would give him a brief comment tonight. Then he said that would be the main topic on the return trip Monday, because we probably would not have the time Sunday. Shortly after the clock chimed eleven, Mr. Adams said he had some legal work that he had to complete and knew we needed our rest. That was a very polite way of telling us that we were sitting in his office and he had to do some work.

I missed my John, but the bed was so comfortable that I was soon sound asleep. Sunday was remarkable, because of all of the things we did and how well we were treated. It was as if slavery had not happened in Braintree and we had been part of the Unitarian church for years. Alex got to play the entire day with children who thought nothing of his black skin. However, there was so much going on that John Adams and I did not have time to talk. That left the ride back to Boston on Monday morning as our best chance to discuss Washington, America, and slavery, along with many other topics.

The Adams' coach was enclosed, but much smaller than the Warren's. Alex curled up in the corner of one side with a book. Just as on the trip down, he did not say a thing until we reached Boston. However, Mr. Adams and I did not stop talking until the coach stopped in front of my Boston home. At that point, I was certain Mr. Adams had a new-found respect for General Washington, and we had both fortified our anti-slavery beliefs. We found out that we had both read many of the same books. As I was disembarking from the coach, Mr. Adams told me that if I ever needed legal assistance, I could call on him.

We arrived in Boston before John got home from work. I could see that he did not eat well while I was gone. I had time to prepare his favorite meal of ham, white beans, slaw, and corn bread and had it ready when he came home. I kept Alex up so he could see his father, but soon it got so late I had to carry a sleeping Alex to his bed. Oh, how I wanted to see my husband. Just three days away from home felt like forever. I fell asleep in my chair dreaming about him.

*To pray unto the most high God,
And beg restraining grace,
Then by the power of his word
You'll see the Saviour's face*

Phillis Wheatley

Chapter 13–Happiness Taken

John told me many times to stay out of the city until the war was over. He reminded me of what happened to my friend Tuck and how easily that could happen to me. Little Alex and I were confined to our apartment and the small community around the apartment. The British had long been gone from Boston, but John knew that many loyalists remained. Then there was the fact that we were an African family. Although free, we could easily be abducted and taken south. Finally, John reminded me that he had been working most recently with what could only be called cruel people. John, however, continued his daily trips into the city. He had to do this in order for us to survive.

Each morning when he left, he held little Alex and me and told us how much he loved us. Although this parting ceremony had been occurring for months now, each time it happened was as intense as the first, and when he came home covered from head to toe with ink, we always took a walk around our block before he cleaned up, with little Alex in tow, and shared our dreams for the future. John talked about returning to the practice of law, and I talked about writing poetry. John laughed as he said only I would notice the ink on his dark skin. He never got home before dark, so even I had trouble seeing the ink that covered every bare spot on his body.

One day, John never came home. I assumed there had been press problems, as seemed to happen five or six times a month. We would not be able to make our little walk, and Alex and I would go ahead with supper. As we ate, I kept waiting for the sound of John climbing the stairs. It's funny how you know who a person is by the sound of their walk. John's sound never came that night.

I did not sleep, and soon the night changed to day. I could not leave Alex, so I carried him with me as I followed John's route home. Because of the war, very few constables were left to take care of the city, and even fewer to work the outer area where we lived. Just as Alex and I started down the path toward town, a gentleman rode up and caught my attention. He asked me if a John Peters lived here, and I told him I was Mrs. Peters. He told me that he was an officer of the law and showed me his badge. He asked if we could go back inside because he had to tell me something.

I knew I was about to hear bad news and only hoped that John was still alive. The man said,

There is no easy way to say this, Mrs. Peters. Your husband is dead. He was the victim of a robbery. You should know that he was hit in the head with one ball and did not suffer."

I could not hold back. My heart was broken. The man comforted a confused Alex, while I began to bear the unbearable news.

The constable said tracks at the site, and the look of the wound, showed the murderer and thief shot my husband at close range, just after he passed by a large bush. The robber took John's life for one week of a printer's pay. We did not have much, but John routinely gave some of his hard earned money to those less fortunate than we were. Although he left this world early, John had done the equivalent of hundreds of years worth of kindnesses. I pray that justice prevails.

As I write about this part of my life, some time has passed and softened the horrible event that took the life of my love. I was able to write eulogies even as I performed slave duties, but I found it impossible to eulogize my John. I was overwhelmed by grief and longed for someone else to perform the noble task of penning John's memorial. There was, however, no one but me who could adequately tell the story of such an inspirational person.

As a Christian, I knew John deprived the devil of a victim as John walked too early into the dust of death. That thought gave me a start on his elegy. I will quote some of the elegy for you now as I write it from memory:

> Grim Monarch! see depriv'd of vital breath,
> A young lawyer in the dust of death!
> Dost thou go on incessant to destroy:
> The grief to double, and impair the joy?
> Enough thou never yet mandate to obey.
> Nor youth, nor science nor the charms of love,
> Nor aught on earth thy rocky heart can move.
> The friend, the spouse, from his dark realm to save.
> In vain we ask the tyrant of the grave.
> Fair mourner, there see thy own John spread,
> Lies undistinguish'd from the vulgar dead;
> Clos'd are his eyes, eternal slumbers keep,
> His senses bound in never-waking sleep,
> Till time shall cease; till many a shining world,
> Shall fall from Heav'n, in dire confusion hurl'd:
> Till dying Nature in wild tortures lies;
> Till her last groans shall rend the brazen skies!
> And not till then, his active Soul shall claim,

Its body, now, of more than mortal frame.
But ah! Methinks the rolling tears apace,
Pursue each other down the alter'd face.
Ah! Cease ye sighs, nor rend the mourner's heart:
Cease thy complaints, no more thy griefs impart.
From the cold shell of his great soul arise!
And look above, thou native of the skies!
There fix thy view, where fleeter than the wind
Thy John flies, and leaves the earth behind.
Thyself prepare to pass the gloomy night,
To join forever in the fields of light;
To thy embrace, his joyful spirit moves,
To thee thy partner of his earthly loves;
He welcomes thee to pleasure more refin'd
And better suited to the deathless mind.

I meant to write only the first line or two, but I could not stop the words once I started writing. I am sure the reader will indulge me this brief lapse into memories of my beloved husband and closest friend. In fact, John is with me as much today as he was when physically present, because of his powerful spiritual image. I even find myself talking with him as if he were standing right next to me. When I talk through a problem with him, I have great confidence in the solution. To this date, that confidence has never been diminished.

Perhaps nothing brings me back to reality more than the thought of having to raise little Alex and pay the bills entirely by myself. I quickly learned that the money I made writing fillers for the newspaper would not handle our needs, but things have a way of working out.

With a small sum of money, I set out to buy John's coffin. There was a small woodworking shop not too far from our apartment. When I walked in, the owner recognized me immediately, and before I could even ask his prices, he told me that he would consider it an honor to give me John's coffin. He told me that he knew me from my writing, but that John had helped him with both money and his strong arms on many occasions. He assured me that the coffin would be ready in time for John's funeral Saturday morning.

There is no way John's help or loans to this man could have equaled to the cost of the coffin he offered me. At this point, I did not even know the woodworker's name, but he could see that I was uneasy. When the woodworker spoke, there was such deep sincerity in his voice, I could not help but wonder why he felt so moved. Then, as if he read my mind, he said,

"Mrs. Peters, believe me, I owe John much more than his coffin. However, you should know that I also have other very personal reasons for doing you this service. I do not know you well, but perhaps over time, I will be able to give you further explanation."

The woodworker was a shy man, and I could tell that he was becoming uncomfortable. I accepted his gift, but told him that when I was able, he would surely get paid for his work. He told me that the coffin had been paid for, and that he needed to begin work immediately in order to have it ready by Saturday.

I took my dismissal cue, but his kind smile also told me that there was more to talk about someday. I found myself in a similar situation at the funeral home. I was very familiar with the funeral home people because I had supplied many a eulogy for their clientele. They told me that there was no way that they could allow me to pay for their services. Finally, the minister would not even allow me to bring up the topic of paying for John's funeral. I went home relieved, humbled, and full of love.

*What deep-felt sorrow in each kindred breast
With keen sensation rends the heart distress'd!
A wife's love sustains a tenderer part,
And morns a Husband with an aching heart*

Phillis Wheatley

Chapter 14—On Our Own

Until I saw the dirt falling on John's coffin, I still felt that he was with me. I knew he could not get out of his coffin, but he still had a presence. The filled grave left me with fond memories and a strong sensation of the spiritual. It is strange how I relate to John, even though he no longer is alive.

The day after the funeral, John's boss, Mr. Jordan, knocked on the apartment door. I opened the door, not expecting to see such an important person. He asked politely if we might talk. I told him we were honored that he would pay us a visit. He immediately started talking about John. He said that although John spent most of his time working on the presses, he had also done legal work for the company. That legal work helped the company move from a twelve-page weekly paper to a ten-page daily. John drew up contracts and did the deed work in the mornings before he started the presses.

"Also," Mr. Jordan went on, "I must have asked his counsel on at least a hundred other company concerns. He never complained or asked for extra pay. He did all of that while keeping the presses running flawlessly. That is why he left so early for work. At the time, we could not afford to hire a law firm. The truth is that without John, I would have lost the business, and because of John, we are a very strong company."

He continued, "Now we employ the best law firm in town. I will not forget when their top lawyer came into my office and asked me the name of our previous attorney. He told me how good his work had been and that they would like to offer him a job. I never told John, for fear that he would no longer run our presses. You see, Mrs. Peters, I owe your husband much more than he was ever paid. I intend to make things right in my heart by offering you a position that will allow you to keep your apartment and feed your family."

He went on, "I also know that you have a young son, so I will give you the time with pay to make arrangements for his care. I have a request for you in that regard. Would you consider allowing an elderly servant from my household to live with you and Alex? I have no idea how old she is, but she is very good with children, having helped raise our three sons. We are going to free her, but she has nowhere to go, though she can continue staying with us. Her name is Miss Sally, and she has been with us for several years. I think the only way to get her to leave is for you to hire her. She often talks about you. You must know that you are a heroine of sorts for Boston slaves. Of course, I will also help with Sally's pay and give her a nice severance amount. I trust you will help her with finances, since she has never had her own money."

Now I know I will be chided for what I am about to write, but I must say it anyway. My John was still watching over his family. Mr. Jordan's offer came from nowhere else but heaven. John kept us from joining the ranks of the needy. Not only did we avoid abject poverty, but we were in a position to thrive. No, you can make fun of me, but you cannot deny what Mr. Jordan said:

"My heart requires that I help you, because I owe John so much."

So anyway you look at it, John helped us.

I took Mr. Jordan's offer without wavering. We decided to ask Miss Sally that evening if she would be willing to live with Alex and me and to watch Alex while I was away at work. Mr. Jordan said,

"It was Sally's custom to eat by herself while we had our meal. She let us know that she would be there in the event we need another servant, which never happens. Like clockwork, she always appears to help clear the table and wash dishes."

That night, instead of beginning dinner, Mr. Jordan, Alex, and I sat down with Sally in the kitchen. She did not know what was happening and seemed scared. Mr. Jordan said,

"Sally, I have a special guest I want you to meet. This lady has talked with General Washington, and her husband saved my business."

Sally looked around, thinking that perhaps we were new slaves for important-looking white people. Also, you could tell by the look on her face she still had no idea why anyone would be introduced to her.

Mr. Jordan said, "Sally, this is Louisa Peters and her son Alex. You probably know her as Louisa Wheatley, as she only recently married John Peters." To my great embarrassment, Sally cried, and uttered at the same time,

"I cannot imagine being in the same room with such a famous person. I do not know what to do or say."

I quickly said, "Sally, my dear, it is our privilege to meet you, but I am here for a very personal reason that can only be described as answered prayer. My husband John was brutally murdered just two days ago. Mr. Jordan has offered me not only a job that will take care of our needs, but also, Sally, he will free you to live with us, if you are willing. I will pay you a fair wage from my earnings and help you adjust to freedom."

Mr. Jordan did not expect me, nor did I expect myself, to blurt out all the words I said, but they were said, and the offer was made. Mr. Jordan broke the silence by assuring Sally that both he and Mrs. Jordan approved of the idea, and he added that she could always return for a visit or to stay with them if things did not work out. He also told her that she would get a good amount of money to open a bank account and that I would help her with all the details.

I knew how Sally felt because I had felt the same way when Mr. Jordan visited me that morning. All Sally could do was cry. I am guessing that she was in her seventies, and there she sat crying like a baby. Then the most precious thing I have ever witnessed happened. Alex walked over to Sally and wrapped his arms around her and said,

"Miss Sally, please help my mother and me, because we need you so much. I promise I will not cause you any trouble. You can have my bed, because I like sleeping on the floor."

Miss Sally said that her little boy would never sleep on the floor. Then she asked my pardon for referring to Alex as her little boy. I told her that it was a compliment for her to have so much love for my son. I told both of them I had already figured out the sleeping arrangements. I am going to make private the bookshelf corner where I have my desk. I can think of no greater pleasure than falling asleep surrounded by my books.

This time, Mrs. Jordan chimed in with an offer of curtains to make a fair-sized room. She told us that she had wanted to replace the drapery in her two front rooms, but did not want the old material wasted. She recalled how difficult it was to get material when she first had the drapery made about fifteen years ago. Since privacy was not an issue in those two rooms, we could have the material right away. She added that in those fifteen years, she never recalled the drapery being shut.

Then, almost magically, the room was silent and we all looked toward Miss Sally, who was just beginning to get back her composure. Through sobs of both joy and sorrow, Miss Sally said, "I will finish my life on this earth living in freedom, because of the kindness of my master and the love of young Alex and his mother. Oh, how the Lord has blessed me. If my master will grant my freedom, and if Miss Louisa and young Alex will have me, then I will gladly go where I think the good Lord is leading me."

Mr. Jordan said the move could easily be made after church services on Sunday, since Miss Sally had so few belongings. Further, he told her that Monday morning before work, they would open a bank account for her. Again, my thoughts turned to John, who must have been smiling as he looked lovingly on us from heaven.

In a period of less than two weeks, I endured the loss of John, but through the grace of God was given a good job and a housekeeper. At one moment, I was as low as a person can get, and then, because of my beloved husband, our family reaped a garden full of blessings. Sally reluctantly moved into my bedroom, and Alex kept his room. I was very happy in the new curtained room with my charming oak desk and a very select collection of books. We bought a small bed that doubled as a settee during the day. To my delight, my bedroom looked more like a library than a place to sleep.

Everything went well. Sally was a Godsend. She loved Alex just as if he were her own son.

I have not mentioned the war for a reason—it would overwhelm this meager story. By now, you know that I am selfish and unable to share my story with the far greater story of the war for independence. Also, from my perspective, it appears we might be losing, and I do not want to write about the possibility of being under control of the British. I know the British to be good people, but, for some reason, they placed impossible tax burdens on these young colonies. I guess the war got into my book, because just a month ago, the British captured Charleston, and that is why I said we might not win the war, but today some very good news came. The new Massachusetts constitution was endorsed, and it states that "all men are born free and equal," and that includes all black people. Also, today, the newspaper got word that we defeated the British in the Battle of Springfield, New Jersey, so perhaps the tide is turning.

I could not believe that I was being paid so well to do what I had done for free in the past. I enjoyed finding out about the people whom death visited. I could always find something nice to put in the paper, and I usually added a short poem as a memorial. I had been producing the entire obituary page for almost three months, and I was beginning to feel secure. I was especially proud of the kind letters the newspaper got, thanking us for the obituary page. Mr. Jordan would bring them to me to read and then post them on a large bulletin board.

I was thankful for the new constitution, because it made it very easy to get Alex into the Boston Free School. The school was in session from eight in the morning until two in the afternoon. That gave Sally six hours to be on her own. She and Alex often made trips during the day, but she seldom got to be on her own. I must admit that I feared Sally would so enjoy her freedom that she would leave us. She somehow sensed my concern and one day asked to talk with me. I just knew she wanted to tell me she had found a better job and place to live. However, I was wrong, and my fears were totally unfounded. What she told me was she never wanted to leave our home. She was worried that I might be jealous of the attention she paid Alex. I assured her that thought had never entered my mind. She said that I paid her too much, and I told her she did not get enough money. After a while, we both stopped talking and hugged each other. Sally laughed as she left the room with the final comment that the only thing that would tear her away from our home was a man as good as my John (God rest his soul).

Alex did well in school. Sally spent most of her time in a school for former slaves. Even as I write this, I still find it hard to believe that someone seventy years old could be like a young schoolgirl. She said simply that age did not matter when you were living your dream.

It was almost as if she did not want Alex to learn more than she learned. Sally was able to learn enough to help Alex with his studies, and I helped both of them on weekends. I usually had newspaper work to do at home during the week and relied on Sally to keep Alex happy.

We all looked forward to Sunday when we put on our best clothes and worshiped with our neighbors at a gray rock church built by the parents of the current congergation. The outstanding feature of this church was the beautiful stained glass windows. By building the church themselves, they were able to put all their money into the windows, and they did a wonderful thing. Our seats are in a perfect place to see each window aglow during the service. Not only are we bathed in the sheer beauty of the church and its windows, but the minister showers us with inspiring sermons. We walk home feeling refreshed and ready for a new week. Alex leaves after the opening prayers and goes to a special children's service that always includes tasty pastries given to us by the best bakery in town. There is an elaborate puppet stage to tell bible stories. The minister works very closely with the people taking care of the children, to see that they get a child's version of the message he is preaching. They cooperate so well that the three of us discuss the Sunday service on the way home, and it is always as if we have heard the same sermon.

I forgot to mention that we come early so we can walk around the church getting an up-close look at each window. Then on the way home, we share a new detail we found in a window and the message for that day. There is never enough time to complete our Sunday discussion. It continues through the week, until we start a new one the following Sunday.

Monday morning found me at my desk getting the day's death notices ready for the typesetter. The Sunday service was still on my mind, and that made me smile. I did not see Mr. Jordan come in, and he startled me with his usual loud,

"And how is Louisa doing?" Before I could speak he added, "You look happy."

There was no way I could explain to him how I felt, so I simply agreed with him and asked him if he needed to see today's writing. I also thought he might be bringing me another letter, but he said,

"I have something to ask you."

Inside, I felt fear, because Mr. Jordan looked so somber. I just knew I had made some awful mistake and my wonderful world was about to be shattered.

Mr. Jordan saw my change and smiled while saying, "Relax, my dear, you are doing a great job. I am here to offer you a promotion. You see, we want to start a column about our community and its people. We think you are the best person to write the column, but we have no one better than you to write death notices. I guess that is why I looked so frightening when I first walked in, because there does not seem to be a solution to this problem.

There is only one Louisa Peters. Then we happened upon what I hope is the answer. The new column would not run daily, but rather, only when you have a column done. That means it could be once a week or once a month, depending on when you have it ready. We want quality, rather than daily summaries of events in the community. At any rate, we will pay you well, if you are willing to do the extra work. We will also provide you with a staff of three people who can do the leg work while you do the writing. I would like to tell you that we will find a replacement for you so you can stop writing death notices and give all of your time to the new column. We will certainly look for that replacement, but the person must be almost as good as you. I say almost, because there will never be anyone found, in my opinion, who writes them as well as you."

He continued, "We did hire a very bright young lady named Mary Hays just yesterday. She is unusual, inasmuch as she provided an obituary as a writing sample. Perhaps with your help, she could develop her obvious writing talent and give you some help with obituaries. So, if you are willing to start a column devoted to Boston life, we will give you all the support we can muster."

At this point, I told Mr. Jordan that I would indeed enjoy the challenge, and that it would not be that difficult for me to keep the obituary page responsibility as well.

"In a way," I said, "I will be like the John Peters we both admire. If you do not mind, I would like to write the first column about the equality statements in the state constitution that Governor John Hancock just helped get passed, and I would like to talk with Mary Hays to see if she has a feeling for writing obituaries. I will be able to tell immediately if she has the proper feelings necessary to honor the departed Boston souls. I will thank you for your generous offer with hard work and dedication. God bless you, Mr. Jordan."

An Elegy, To Miss Mary Moorhead, on the death of her Father, The Rev. Mr. John Moorehead

But cease complaining, hush each murm'ring tongue,
Pursue the Example which inspires my Song,
Let his Example in your Conduct shine;
Own the afflicting Providence, divine;
So shall bright Periods grace your joyful Days,
And heavenly Anthems swell your Songs of Praise.

Phillis Wheatley

Chapter 15—A New Beginning

I could not believe my good fortune. In just a few months, without any effort on my part, my life was secure, and I was being paid a handsome salary to write. Mr. Jordan gave Mary an entire week to find out if she could handle the obituary page with minimal help from me. In a way, I was hurt when her first effort was every bit as good as anything I could write. Then we had to go out and seek information about a young man named John Eccles when word got to us that he had died of a fever. Eccles had been involved in local politics, but had no relatives in Boston. Mary did all the work as I observed. After talking with his landlord, minister, and barber, she had enough information to write a dignified and informative obituary.

There was no need to worry. I knew Mary would do well and that she would seldom need my help. The week we spent together was like a vacation for me. I told Mr.

Jordan on Monday that Mary could do the job, and I could start on my new assignment, but he insisted we take the entire week. It was only necessary to read over Mary's work, checking for accuracy, since she was not yet that familiar with our area of Boston. I never found any punctuation or grammar mistake in her writing. I could relax because I knew the obituaries would not lessen in quality with Mary in charge. When Mary told me that writing the last words about a person was both rewarding and interesting work, I knew she would be with us for awhile. Those who look at it as a chore soon tire, because people die every day, and so your chore is never complete, while those of us who find joy in what we do look forward to each day. Mary Hays, like me, felt great joy penning soothing remarks for those in the throes of grief.

As promised, the next week, Mr. Jordan gave me a sizable room to outfit for the production of a new column. There was a supply of furniture in a warehouse a short distance from the newspaper. Anything stored there was ours to use, and also we could order furniture designed from the local cabinetmaker. When my three assistants arrived, we would all go to the warehouse to select furniture for the new "Boston Report" newsroom. I was mentally arranging the room when three strange men walked in. Without even an introduction, one of them told me to go get them some tea because they had to wait for a new editor. They said writers like themselves deserved good service and might even give me a tip if I performed well for them. They joked with each other that, because the new editor was a woman, they had better get used to her being late. The way they talked without acknowledging my presence brought back my slave days waiting table for the Wheatleys.

I said not a word, but went to the tea room and brought back four hot pots of tea. By then, the men had improvised a table and three seats. It was obvious that they thought highly of themselves. One scolded me rather severely, because I had a fourth teapot on the tray. I could not speak fast enough to put a stop to what I knew would embarrass them. They were enjoying their power. As soon as one finished the fourth-cup tirade, another scolded me for not curtseying after taking their orders. Just then, Mr. Jordan appeared. They quickly offered Mr. Jordan my pot of tea and tried to impress him by telling him they had anticipated his arrival and had the tea brewed just for him. Mr. Jordan said that was very strange, because he had no intention of coming by so soon, but just happened to be in this part of the building. Then he looked at me and asked why I did not have a cup of tea. I told him that I would get a cup later, and then noticed the sheepish looks on the faces of the men.

I said not a word as Mr. Jordan openly told me how he had picked three good writers to help me get the new column started. He said that, since we had already met, he would forgo introductions. As is his character, he described a weakness in each man saying that, with my help, they would be able to improve. He finished his tea and then told me that he had to leave immediately for a lunch date with Governor Hancock. I reminded him that I wanted the first column to be about the equality statements in the new constitution and asked if he could arrange for an interview for me with the Governor. He said he would do just that, and it would probably be tomorrow, because the Governor was also anxious to get out information about the constitution. As we talked business, no attention was given the three men. Finally, Mr. Jordan took his leave, and only then did he acknowledge the three men with these words:

"Do exactly as Mrs. Peters tells you, because she is by far the best writer in Boston."

I walked Mr. Jordan to the door and thanked him again for the job and all of his help. He simply said to me that he was the one who should be giving thanks. I could say nothing, but, by the looks we exchanged, I knew this venture would be a success. Turning to come back to where the three men were standing, I could see absolute dismay on their faces. In fact, they looked so depressed that it was comical.

I put them somewhat at ease when I burst into laughter, but still the three men stood before me shoulder to shoulder in a sad pose fitting for the gallows, rather than esteemed writers. Before one of them could get out the words, "How can we apologize?" I said,

"Forget what happened, because I assure you that I will."

I did not know their names, so I said,

"Mr. Jordan told me your writing needs, but failed to tell me your names. Do you mind introducing yourselves, along with some personal information?"

There was silence. I now know that it was very difficult for the men to accept my being both a woman and from Africa. Back then, I had too much on my mind to even think about social problems. A man named Andrew Bradford clumsily talked first. He said that he had been in the newspaper business since he was eight years old, when he sold newspapers on a corner not far from this building. He told me he was married, with two children, and was a Harvard graduate. Andrew was a young, ruggedly handsome blond whose good looks drew you to him.

Alan Spector spoke next. He was also a Harvard graduate, married with one child. Alan was short and stocky, and this was his first real work experience. His family and his wife's family took care of their needs while he was in school.

Then Sam Pope introduced himself as being not married and not having graduated from college. His life was the newspaper and, like my husband, he was able to set up and run a press. Sam was tall and very thin. He was not good-looking, but had an endearing quality about him that made you enjoy his being there. Only recently had Sam done any writing, but it was good enough to get Mr. Jordan's attention. Also, Sam could fix anything. Andrew was also good with tools, but Alan did not even know how to use a screwdriver.

Andrew, Alan, and Sam would be forever grateful to me for not having embarrassed them in front of Mr. Jordan. I thanked them for volunteering for the "Boston Report" assignment and then told them about myself. Sam had personal knowledge of my John's skills, as John had helped him out with a press problem just a few weeks before John was murdered. Sam said the press was over-inking and everything he tried had failed. John fixed the thing in just an hour, and it has worked well since. Andrew and Alan knew about my writing and the trip I made to England. While I was talking with Andrew and Alan, Sam slipped out and got me a cup of tea.

It was lunch time. I usually ate some crackers, a slice of cheese, and whatever fruit we had, because I did not have the money to buy lunch. I told my new co-workers that we would meet at the warehouse at 2 p.m. to select furniture for our office. I knew they would eat at the restaurant frequented by the press. John had eaten there once and told me about it for months afterward. They insisted that I go with them and that they would pay for my meal. I agreed when they said the warehouse was close to the restaurant, and that by eating together we could probably be picking out furniture by 1 p.m.

As I looked at the list of food items written with chalk on a large slate, the image of John eating there came to mind. In fact, Mr. Jordan had bought his meal because he stayed after work to get out a late edition. The words, "Your order, Ma'am," brought me out of my dream, and the meal John talked about for a month poured from my mouth. I ordered a small portion of cured ham, baked beans, fall squash, a slice of bread, and a glass of pear cider. John particularly praised the bread, beans, and cider, but concluded that the ham was the best he had ever eaten. I will be forever grateful to my new friends for making it possible to eat this most meaningful meal that brought back so clearly the experience of my beloved John. The wonderful food allowed me to savor in much more detail one of John's last stories.

I think we were all excited to start the project, because we finished lunch and were on the way to the warehouse a little bit before 1 p.m. As we walked, we talked about the furniture we needed. Each of us would look for a desk. We also agreed to get a big table for meetings. Chairs for that table would serve as guest chairs, if we had a visitor at our desk. We would need some cabinets to keep things on which we were working.

There were workers at the newspaper who did nothing but catalog and store things for the writers. I was already familiar with their work because they often helped me when I wrote an obituary.

We soon reached the warehouse and were overwhelmed by how much furniture was neatly stacked along its walls and aisles. The men all picked large, lavish desks, but I found a small, well-made one with many compartments. The desk was made with burled wood, and showed character. I figured it would be a joy to work on it, and if I needed more room, I would use the big table.

It was funny how we all settled on the big table. All of us were looking for a desk when, at the same time, we sighted a beautiful dark table surrounded by handsome leather-covered chairs. We came out from searching the rows of desks at the same time and lined up around this table without noticing each other. We were so taken with the table's beauty that we failed to see each other. Then, almost as if it had been planned, we rubbed our hands across the dusty top to expose the beautiful wood underneath. Seeing each other for the first time, we broke out in laughter, and agreement came quickly. We happily put tags on it and all the chairs. We could see ourselves around the table working on the column.

The need to find cabinets quickly ended the dreaming. Surprisingly, what we thought would be the most difficult furniture to find proved the easiest. The man in charge of the warehouse came back to check on us, and we told him we were looking for cabinets. He took us to yet another section of the warehouse and started telling us the stories behind each stored piece. I paid little attention to him, thinking that this might be the time to use our other option of having the cabinets built, but then I heard the words "large, North-end room" and saw just what we needed. Indeed, he said the cabinets were custom-made for the first managing editor's room that was gutted when the new addition was added to an already large building.

It seems that, until recently, what was to become the office for the "Boston Report" column had been used for newsprint storage. We had found the very cabinets that were built for the managing editor of the newspaper. They would be a perfect fit, and we outfitted the entire room without spending any new money. No doubt Mr. Jordan would be happy, although there is no telling how much money he made because everyone in Boston, rich or poor, bought the paper.

The warehouseman told us the furniture would be delivered and installed the next day. He was happy to free up the space, and we were pleased to get such fine furnishings.

Without any furniture we could not do any newspaper work, but we decided to go back to the office and give it a thorough cleaning while it was empty. We put in two hours of sweeping, scrubbing, and polishing before calling it a day. It was agreed that we would all arrive at six the next morning to make preparation before the furniture came. As I walked home on the same path my beloved John had taken so many times, I thought to myself how happy he must be.

You should also know that I had three escorts for my short trip. Andrew, Alan, and Sam insisted on walking me home. They told me that there would never be a night that at least one of them did not accompany me. Nothing I said would change their minds, so I agreed, providing that I would be responsible for brewing and maintaining our stock of tea. They agreed, knowing that I did not want in any way to even appear to be taking advantage of my position. The four of us used these walks to plan the next day. The invigorating harbor breeze would wash over us for about three blocks, and then, just past King's Chapel, we came to my apartment, with a huge oak tree growing in the front. If we happened to be walking at six, the huge Chapel bell would ring for us. On looking back, I know these evening walks were in some measure responsible for the success of the "Boston Report." Perhaps the greatest benefit of our walks was I could spend the rest of the night enjoying Alex, knowing that the next morning was already planned. Nothing can compare to the big hug waiting for me at the top of the stairs. I am truly blessed.

Hymn to Humanity

*Each human Heart inspire
To act in Bounties unconfin'd
Enlarge the close contracted Mind,
And fill it with sacred Fire.*

Phillis Wheatley

Chapter 16—Our First Article

I forgot that I asked Mr. Jordan to arrange a meeting with Governor Hancock. Have you ever noticed that often when you think about someone, that person pays you a visit? It makes you think the visit happened because you were thinking about the person.

They delivered my desk first, I suppose, because it was the smallest. I was so busy putting supplies in my desk that I did not notice Mr. Jordan standing behind me. When I finally turned around, the imposing figure standing so close to me caused a startled sound that caught the attention of everybody in the room. Mr. Jordan reacted to the noise by flinching. Then there was a long pause; at least, it seemed like a long pause, as we both regained our composure.

I felt a tingling sensation as the blood ran to my face. I was glad my dark skin hid my embarrassment, but before I could get an apology out of my mouth, Mr. Jordan told me how sorry he was for frightening me so. Not to dwell on what made us both uncomfortable, he quickly told me that I was using his old desk. He said it was providential that I picked his old desk out of the hundreds of desks stored in the warehouse. For him, this was a sign that it was God's will that led him to hire me, a former slave, to write such an important column. I guess the scare put him in a talkative mood, because he allowed that, had he not been adopted by a wealthy uncle, he would not be the owner of the most popular newspaper in Boston today. Then he reached into his coat pocket and handed me a sealed note from Governor Hancock, with whom he had had lunch yesterday.

I could tell that he was torn between telling me more about himself and keeping a demanding schedule. He told me to use the newspaper courier to reply to the Governor and then walked over and greeted Andrew, Alan, and Sam before leaving.

No sooner had Mr. Jordan left than the rest of our furniture started arriving. It seems the word had traveled fast about the new column, and the warehousemen got extra help so our office would get supplies and furniture without delay. Andrew assured me they could handle getting the furniture and setting up the place. They knew I wanted to read and answer the Governor's letter. Sitting down at my desk for the first time, I stared at the wax seal too beautiful to break. Just a drop of candle wax would seal my return message.

I wondered how the Governor found time to visit with Mr. Jordan and write such a lengthy message. He said that he would be honored by my visit, but hoped that his proposed meeting place would be suitable. He had been to a few of my poetry sessions at the Bradford Tavern and suggested our meeting take place there. He assured me that we would get more done at the Tavern than in his office. The note said that, since becoming Governor, he had not been able to visit a tavern, and he thought our meeting there would allow both of us to relax and be forthcoming about the important issue of equality. He heard that the Bradford Tavern had just gotten a shipment of Perry (pear cider). He had not tasted any in over a year. He said something about the best popcorn in Boston, but closed by saying he would also be happy to have an office meeting if I preferred.

I told him that I would enjoy meeting in the Tavern rather than his office and that I, too, enjoyed Perry, having drunk it in English pubs with Dr. Franklin. I am sure the British mixed apple and pear cider together for practical reasons, but the result was a delightful taste that seemed to linger longer than any other cider. Having a glass of this year's Perry was reason enough to meet at the pub.

I must digress a moment. Reading over my manuscript, I realized that the last few chapters would make you believe that the war had been over for years. The truth is that the end came just a little over a year ago. You might also think that I have forsaken writing poetry for my newspaper work. Perhaps a few lines of my latest poem will let you know both that I still write poems and that I am keenly aware of the just-won war setting my country free. Oh, how I love freedom. I call this poem "Liberty and Peace," and I am going to share the first eight lines:

> Lo! Freedom comes. Th' prescient Muse foretold,
> All Eyes th' accomplish'd Prophecy behold:
> Her Port describ'd, "She moves divinely fair,
> Olive and Laurel bind her golden Hair."
> She, the bright Progeny of Heaven, descends,
> And every Grace her sovereign Step attends;
> For now kind Heaven, indulgent to our Prayer,
> In smiling Peace resolve the Din of War.

Now I hope that taste of poetry in the midst of prose will cause you to seek out the rest of the poem. So much good has happened to me that, in this book, at least, my personal delight seems to have overshadowed the birth of a nation. Historians, no doubt, will record the recent memorable events much better than this poet-turned-columnist. I ask my reader to be content with my telling of my personal story, that is also unique in history. I gained my freedom about the same time as this country. Just a few years ago, I was property, and now, I am on the verge of becoming a Boston newspaper columnist.

Returning to my story, I think it grand that the Governor trusted me enough to ask for the pub meeting. Actually, I wondered how he knew how much I loved to visit the pub, and to be able to go to the pub with such distinguished company intensified my appreciation for Governor Hancock. In this section of Boston, my black skin was not an impediment. It was very similar to the treatment I got in London. The appointed time was the next day at 2 p.m. I knew that there would not be many people in the pub at that time so we would probably have a good deal of privacy until around 4 p.m. An hour or two with such a remarkable man is all that I could want.

It was funny when we entered the pub, because the couple at the door, old friends named Sean and Katie Keel, greeted the governor by saying,

"John, it has been at least a year since we've seen you."

In his note, the governor had made it very clear how much he enjoyed the pub and how long it had been since he had been able to visit the place, and the Keels immediately made note of how long it had been since they had seen the man they remembered as simply John, but who was now the governor. Then they looked at me and said,

"Louisa, will we be privileged to hear one your poems today?"

I had no time to reply, because in the next breath, they said they were looking forward to the new column.

Obviously, the Keels did not grasp the import of having the governor dine in their pub. For them, this was just two old friends returning after being away for a long time. Both the governor and I valued that outlook and the relaxed, friendly feeling of the pub. It turned out that neither I nor the governor had eaten breakfast that morning, and both of us were hungry. Katie brought our cider, then suggested that we celebrate our return with a special, Irish meal. She told us that the cider would be perfect with what they were about to fix. The Keels wanted us just to sit back and enjoy their hospitality, and we readily agreed.

I was mistaken when I wrote that the Keels did not know the importance of having the governor eat in their pub. They fixed a meal that was the tastiest food I have ever eaten. Only the Irish can fry onions and potatoes and braise cabbage with such skill. The amazing thing was that he took into account that we would all be eating supper in just a few hours after leaving their place, so the food was great, but the proportions did not leave us unable to eat properly with our families later that night. As we were eating, Sean started carving a sign that he said would be nailed to the wall right above our table. It will read, "Governor John Hancock and writer Louisa Peters ate here on April 15, 1785."

As Sean brought out a dish of young venison, I got to the meat of my discussion with the governor. I asked him directly why he was so concerned about equality. I also wanted to know why he would risk his political career by sponsoring a law that gave Africans the same rights as white people. Even in Boston, most of the people thought of Africans as subhuman. Then I had to tell him that some Africans would be unable to make use of equality because they had not adapted to this country. I told him that the blunders of a few Africans would no doubt be used as a political weapon against him. I had to know if he was prepared for the bad reactions his equality law would bring.

Governor Hancock listened to my questions politely. These issues were so important to me that I realized I had raised my voice like a begging child as I asked my questions. I was glad that the pub was nearly empty, but looking around I saw hurt faces on the patrons. I made myself uncomfortable, so I can only imagine how the governor must have felt, but he did not answer with the same emotion. Instead, he talked with a soothing, even voice, so that I had to hear his words instead of his feelings.

First, he said the Lord gifted him with the good sense to know that hate was intolerable. He said that the real chains of slavery bound those people who thought they were superior because of the color of their skin. Then the governor quoted 1 John 3:14: "He that loveth not his brother abideth in death" and 1 John 4:11: "Beloved, if God so loved us, we ought also to love one another." The Scripture quotes caught me off guard. I did not expect the conversation to come so quickly to Godly matters. Stopping for a moment, perhaps sensing my concern about putting Scripture quotes in the secular press, he said,

"Louisa, if we are unable to call everyone 'brother' then brotherhood does not exist." Then he quoted Scripture again, saying, "He that saith he is in the light, yet hateth his brother, is in darkness even until now." I think that is 1 John 2:9, but please check before you quote me.

I told him that I had just begun working for the newspaper and that I was not sure about using any of his Scripture quotes as part of the column.

"I will say instead that your feelings for equality rise from a deep belief in biblical truths," I said, and he was satisfied with the way I proposed to handle his Biblical quotes. I then told him about my meeting with General Washington, and that the General promised to release his slaves on his death because he also thought that all men were equal. The governor quickly asked why the slaves were not immediately set free, and I explained that the general was also practical, and knew that such a move would be harmful to him, and perhaps even the slaves. General Washington's slaves were treated well. I also told him that the General's wife thought just the opposite of her husband and would not release her slaves for any reason.

Governor Hancock told me about the trouble with John Adams' first draft of our constitution. He said it was much like the differences between George and Martha Washington. Over half of the members had slaves and, when they read Adams' words that "All men are born free and equal," they knew that signing the document would set their slaves free. There were also those among them that had indentured servants who had up to the full seven years to serve before they earned their freedom.

The governor said, "And, before I forget it, Louisa, how do you feel about the second article?"

I had to think a moment, and then I told the Governor that I thought it was essential that we include the worship of God as both a right and a duty. He then asked me why I was so worried about using his Scripture quotes, because we have a right to profess our sentiments.

Further, he said, "There is no way printing Scripture should disturb the public peace, as long as you make it clear that I do not think all people must believe the way I believe."

I could not argue with him, because I felt the same way. However, I did not want to write something that would cause Mr. Jordan trouble, so I asked again if I could just say "strong beliefs" without the quotes, and the Governor gave permission a second time. His words said I could write it my way, but the look he gave me dared me to use the quotes.

The time was approaching 4 p.m., and I knew the Governor had to return to work, so I told him that I had enough material to write the first column. I also said that it was fitting that the first column be about such an important person and what I knew would be a historical document. My words made the Governor uncomfortable, but my turn was next. Sean came to our table and told us that it had been an honor for us to dine at his pub, and there would be no charge for the food. Then he asked me if I would recite just one poem before we left. The pub was beginning to fill, and there was now a sizable crowd in the place. Then the Governor said that it would be a wonderful and fitting way to end this event if I would do such a pleasing thing.

I had to agree, with both the Governor and Sean asking me to perform. As I went up onto the little stage, I had used so many times just a few years ago, some people recognized me and began clapping. I recited my poem, "Liberty and Peace", and then told everyone that I had to get back to work. I promised Sean that I would find the time to recite poetry in a month or two. He understood how important my job was and told me they would look forward to my return. Perhaps, he suggested, I could bring my family with me and just stay no more than an hour. I told him that I would be back, and as the Governor and I left, applause broke out in the pub.

A carriage awaited us. It was just a short distance from the pub to the newspaper, but the Governor insisted that we ride in the carriage. He told me that he would pay Mr. Jordan a brief visit before returning to the State House where several hours of work awaited him. Just as the bells chimed five times, I saw the carriage leave for Beacon Hill. I felt sorry for Governor Hancock, because I knew he would be working until dark to make up for the time he spent with me and Mr. Jordan. I will take my work home tonight and write after Alex falls asleep. I should have the article ready for Andrew and Adam to proof tomorrow morning. By noon, Sam should be setting the type on our first column.

The men had spent the entire day organizing the files and getting background information on the constitution. They were anxious to get my draft in the morning and write the column for the Sunday edition. It would be Andrew and Adam walking me home tonight because Sam wanted to do some more arranging with the type, so that no time would be wasted tomorrow. The bells tolled the half hour, and I knew I would just have to get up and leave. I had promised myself that I would always spend at least three hours with Alex every evening and at least one full day every weekend. By the time we reached my door, we knew exactly how the next day would start. Alex was hugging me before I got to the first step, and, for now, my work was forgotten.

*...thy infinite wisdom
can bring a clean thing out of an
unclean, a vessel of Honor filled
for thy glory—grant me
to live a life of gratitude to thee
for the innumerable benefits*

Phillis Wheately
Excerpt from Prayer
Sabbath—June 13, 1779

Chapter 17—The First Column

Alex and I enjoyed our time together after eating Miss Sally's delicious meal. Alex had the same love of books that John and I shared. He was already reading. I found out that he was helping Miss Sally with her schoolwork during the day. For many years, I read to him before bed, but now he would start the story and then, as he grew tired, he would hand me the book, and I would read until his eyes closed. When I got home the next day, Alex would have read the story from the point he fell asleep and delight in telling me the conclusion.

Miss Sally was knitting a sweater and humming when I sat down to relax before starting the column. Without looking up from her knitting, she told me how much she appreciated being part of our home. I told her that I could not work without her and that it was I who was appreciative. Miss Sally then quite profoundly said her contentment was due to how she felt inside, rather than how nice a life she has now. Sally let me know that she knew Alex and I shared those same feelings. I could only agree with her.

There was a brief silence as we both thought about the words we just said. Then Sally told me that Alex was teaching her to read. I told her that I would also like to help her. She thanked me, but said she knew that I did not have the time. Sally began to struggle for words.

"I hope you understand what I am about to say, because I do not want to offend you," she said. "I share the good feelings I see in Alex's face after I am able to read a page without stumbling. Not that you would not feel the same way, but there is something special when you see that look on a child."

We shared some more pleasantries, and then Sally, anticipating my need to write, told me it was her bedtime. Tonight, she was going to read a few pages first, so she asked me to check the candle before I went to bed. We did not allow Alex to burn his candle before bed. I must buy some of Mr. Revere's lanterns for our bedrooms. They give off plenty of light, and, being enclosed, there is no danger of fire. In fact, his shop is not too far from my work, so I will make it a point to bring some home tomorrow. Then we can all enjoy the pleasure of reading in bed without the worry of setting fire to our home.

Now is my writing time. Surrounded by books, I recalled the days I had only scrap paper and used quills, but now I have a stack of new paper—even a fancy Bion pen. The Bion is beautifully engraved and works very well. Mr. Jordan bought me one for the office and one for my home. The metal nib stays sharp, and the flow of ink makes perfect letters. Well, nearly perfect, I should say. Some letters run together, if I am not careful, but they are still readable by me and, hopefully, the typesetters. He got the pens on his last trip to France, thinking they would be ideal for his editors. We still keep a supply of quills and ink wells, because Bions are just too expensive for everyday use.

While I am talking about my writing equipment, I want you to know that the "Boston Report" has an attractive seal used when we send the final copy to the press room. Because we do so much writing, we also have what I can only describe as a quill on top of a quill. The top quill holds a supply of ink that you gently squeeze to move down into the bottom quill and the writing point. Mr. Jordan is so considerate. He makes it as easy as possible to get our thoughts onto paper. He treats everyone well, not just the writers, but he seems to have a special affinity for us.

As editor, I allow all of us to have rewrite authority, with final approval coming back to me. On the first and second rough copies, we would put our suggestions in parentheses and allow the writer to decide on making the change. As the editor, I could make changes even to the final copy. My byline would go on every column, so I had to be able to defend every word. On articles on which I was not the primary writer, my name would be second. I thought the practice might be a little difficult for Andrew and Adam, since they had graduated from college and I had not, but they never complained.

I heard the bell chime the half-hour, and not a word appeared on my paper. I was putting myself under undue pressure because I had all of tomorrow to work on the column, but I was assuming I would have no interruptions which, even though I had only been a few days on the job, I knew was unlikely. I also thought that, since I was the lead writer for our first column, I should set the example and bring at least a rough draft to work tomorrow.

Being too keyed-up to sleep, I decided to read my notes again. Just as I finished the last page, the bells struck ten times. Almost an hour had gone by, and my paper was still blank. This was a new and bad experience for me. Then my old friend Benjamin Franklin helped me out.

I recalled one night in England as we sat drinking ale at a quaint corner pub, Franklin turned to me and said,

"The noblest question in the world is, 'What good may I do in it?'"

We had been talking about how America was going to change, and what would bring about that change. Mr. Franklin said that there were many good men and women in America, and our country was not bogged down by petty politics. Oh, there were some politics, but not the kind that killed constructive change. He pointed out how better my life was, because the leaders in Boston wanted to do good things for all people. Then I remembered him citing John Hancock as an example of what he was saying.

The jam was broken, and words began to flow. Soon, one page was done. Mr. Jordan wanted the column to be about 750 words long, so I needed another 600 words. I read back over the page and began to worry about using Mr. Franklin's name, because he did have critics in Boston, but I think one reason Mr. Jordan picked me for this job is because he knew I had such friends as Mr. Franklin. I left the quote in the article knowing that Andrew, Adam, or Sam could take it out. True to my word, I did not quote Scripture, but made reference to Governor Hancock's strong beliefs.

Perhaps the most difficult part of writing this first column was keeping my strong feelings of equality out of it. The Governor and I thought so much alike about equality that I had to guard against completing his thought with my own. By the time the bells rang eleven times, I had filled eight pages. I was still not the least bit sleepy. I began to read back through the rough draft, making corrections and additions. Soon, every page had so many changes that it looked horrible. The rough draft would have to be recopied just to be able to read the thing. By now, I was beginning to feel ready for bed and was pleased with my work. Tomorrow I would recopy the pages and pass them to the men for their approval. We would lose Adam at noon, because he was going to start work on the next column about the plans for a new state house.

When I heard twelve chimes, I knew I had to go to bed, even if I couldn't sleep. Tomorrow was Friday, and we worked only a half-day on Saturday, so I lay there thinking about being with Alex and Sally on the weekend. The half-hour tolled, and I could only wonder when sleep would overtake me. I heard a noise outside, and it did not sound too far from our stoop. I went over to the window and peeped out from the bottom corner. Three men from the night watch encircled a man who appeared to have a gun in his hand. I could hear them trying to talk the man into dropping his weapon. Then the man with the gun spoke clearly, saying,

"I killed John, and his wife is next. John took my job, and now his wife is keeping good people from working."

I was thankful that the noise had not awakened Alex or Sally. I watched as the gunman held the three watchmen at bay, while moving toward a horse tied up just past the big oak. He reached the horse and was trying to mount while keeping his gun pointed at the watchmen. Just like that, his horse bolted and spun him around giving the watchmen time to draw their pistols. Three loud cracks pierced the night, and I saw the gunman drop. A watchman fell to a kneeling position. Sally came into the room holding a lantern and asked me what was happening. Next came Alex, hollering, "Mommy, mommy!" I grabbed him up and held him to my breast. I told him everything was fine and not to worry, that three watchmen had just taken care of a bad man, and now everything was back to normal. He wanted to know what the bad man had done, but I did not want to tell him what I had heard. I said I did not know. I was telling the truth, because I had not talked with the watchmen.

A paid law enforcement officer knocked on our door. I could tell he was a constable because of his uniform. The night watch had special caps, but the paid officers had uniforms. He told me what had happened and that there would be no more problems. Alex and Sally were sitting in the room with me, so they heard every word. The officer told me that a very troubled former employee of the newspaper had killed John and wanted to kill me. The man was a heavy drinker and that led to his being unable to do his work and eventually to being fired. He had taken particular offense at being replaced by an African. A member of the night watch had heard him talk about killing John, but the man often talked like that when he had too much to drink. The night watch had kept an eye on the man ever since John's death. They knew he was full of hate and could harm someone else. The officer said the gunman gave a full confession on the street before succumbing to the shots fired by the night watch.

"Mrs. Peters," he said, "I know you have been through a lot these last two months, and tonight was awful, but your troubles, at least with this bloke, are over."

My eyes finally shut sometime after the church bells tolled three times. I was so excited about the first column that I got up early and was at work before anyone else arrived. I was glad that I had spent the time writing that first column last night. Most of the morning was spent with the crime reporter, putting together a report about what had taken place in front of my apartment. Since there was a connection to this newspaper, Mr. Jordan was caught up with the reporting and writing. He was also in our office, and so I had to play the role of hostess. I had to let the men take care of the column.

Andrew, Adam, and Sam made copies from my horrible scratching. I could tell they were having trouble reading my writing, but every time I tried to get involved they would tell me that this was a good trial, and they needed to do the work without my help. Just as I was about to use my authority and take over the copywriting job, Mr. Jordan walked over and embraced me before saying a word.

He held onto me and repeated over and over again, "I hired a madman." As gently as I could, I asked Mr. Jordan to sit down so we could talk. In the newspaper building, there is no privacy. I have a desk and space, but no private office, but I did not care if the men heard what I was about to say. I told Mr. Jordan that the man we now know as Tom Perkins made a good impression and was not drinking at the time of his hire. We also know that something changed his character about six months after he was hired. He eventually got so bad that Mr. Jordan had to fire him. I told Mr. Jordan that I did not think Mr. Perkins himself was guilty. I think something happened inside his head that totally changed him.

"He was not capable of being the person you knew when you hired him," I said, and I began to shake as I told him about seeing men go mad on the slave ship. Then I once again used something my friend Mr. Franklin said, "After crosses and losses, men grow humbler and wiser." I knew that fear was gnawing at Mr. Jordan, but I could see him glow when he finally realized the problem had been taken care of and there would be a brighter tomorrow.

My next move was to get Mr. Jordan back on regular newspaper business. I did this by telling him the "Boston Report" would do at least two, and maybe three, stories on the night watch and the paid law enforcement officers. I could see his eyes sparkle again. Both of us were very proud of Boston and our city government. Mr. Jordan said he would personally verify that Boston was the first city to pay people to keep watch over her citizens. It was the combination of the paid workers and the volunteer night watch that had saved my life. Mr. Jordan asked if he could be the guest writer for this column, and I readily agreed. I told him that, after all, he owned the newspaper. He then reminded me of his promise to never interfere with our column. So, being a man of his word, he did the proper thing by asking me, rather than telling me, that he wished to write the column. I also knew that Mr. Jordan wanted to write the column in such a way as to make amends for even being remotely connected to these two tragedies.

The column on equality caused people to write letters to the paper, and that made Mr. Jordan happy. Most of the letters supported the column, but there were a few negative ones as well. We were so busy that before we knew it we had the makings of enough columns to get us through the year. I began to think Mr. Jordan put too many people to work on the "Boston Report," but now I know that he had other plans. He wanted to make sure the new column succeeded, but he was not averse to asking people to take special assignments.

One day, he showed up a little before noon and asked Sam and me to be his guests at what he called a "working lunch." Before we left, he called all of us together for a special meeting. Mr. Jordan told us how proud he was of our work and that he was especially pleased that we had columns written in advance. Then he said that he wanted to send Sam and me on a special assignment, which he would explain to us at lunch, but before he did that, he wanted to make sure that Andrew and Adam were comfortable running the "Boston Report" room for the next month or two. Both Andrew and Adam said that would not be a problem, and they felt honored that Mr. Jordan trusted them to do the work. That said, we left immediately for lunch. Mr. Jordan told Andrew and Adam that we would give them all the details when we got back.

Mr. Jordan started the conversation in the carriage. He told us about friends of his, the Whitneys, who lived in Westboro. In particular, he talked about their son named Eli. Eli had just started at Yale and was working on a degree in engineering. The Whitneys owned a cotton plantation in South Carolina, and young Eli spent more time there than in school. He knew it was going to take him a long time to get through school, but that was not a problem. He liked farming and made a lot of money, so a college degree was not important to Eli. His parents, however, wanted him to finish college. So Eli would spend the winter months in college and the rest of the time on the plantation. He managed to bring a part of plantation life to Yale. He spent a lot of time in the engineering laboratory working on an invention that would clean cotton. He got the idea from a slave on his plantation. Since the slave was his property, there was no need to pay the slave for his idea.

We arrived at the restaurant, and I wondered why Mr. Jordan had spent the entire time talking about Eli Whitney and what that had to do with the special assignment. None of us ordered a heavy meal because we were more interested in the special assignment than in eating. Mr. Jordan asked me if I had a brother, and I replied, "Yes." He told me that Mr. Wheatley was not a close friend of his, but that because they were both Boston businessmen, it was not uncommon for them to be at a meeting together. Mr. Jordan remembered Mr. Wheatley talking about his newly bought slave girl and how he wished he had gotten her brother instead. He said if he had a hard-working man with my intelligence it would be worth whatever price the trader asked. Further, he recalled my being from Senegal. By this time, I was confused and excited. None of what Mr. Jordan had talked about related to writing the "Boston Report" column. However, he seemed to be saying that my brother was in America.

Mr. Jordan said Eli told his parents that a slave on their South Carolina plantation made a small cotton cleaner. According to Eli, the slave used old horse brushes, various gears, wheels, and belts to make a contraption that removed cotton seed from bolls. The slave's invention was small, but only because he did not have the materials to make a large machine. Eli said that just cranking the handle brings cotton bolls between two sliding brushes that take out all of the seeds and leave clean cotton fibers behind. As soon as the cotton is picked this year, Eli is going to give the slave the materials to build a large cotton-cleaning machine. Several sacks of raw cotton were saved to test the large machine. Eli brought the small machine to school with him so he could start the patent process. Of course, he will get the patent in his name. The slave will get nothing. Eli thinks it will take several years to build a machine able to clean acres of cotton. The legal work could take as much as ten years to finish. There will be a fortune to be made if everything works right. Eli plans to ask for two-fifths of the crop as payment for removing the seed. Mr. Jordan asked us if we had any questions about what he told us. Sam and I both replied." No." Then we both said that the slave was not treated fairly, and Mr. Jordan agreed. Perhaps, he said, your writing might cause the public to feel the same way.

Mr. Jordan, with his hands clasped behind his back, stared out the window before returning his gaze to us. Then he said,

"Now, I know you are wondering where I am going with all my talk about Eli, the invention, and South Carolina. Well, I want to give the public more than just news coverage. I want to take them where it would be impossible for the average citizen to go, and I am not talking about a travelogue. I want to print something that will spark human interest, and I think you two are just the pair to accomplish at least part of my desire."

Looking at Sam's face, I could tell that he was still as confused as I was. Then things cleared up for me when Mr. Jordan said the most astounding thing. He told me that he had a very strong feeling that the slave on the Whitney's plantation was my brother. Mr. Jordan had found out that the slave in question was bought just a few days after me, and that he came from the same area of Senegal that I came from. Now, he knew this was a long shot, but the last factor, his intelligence, seemed to confirm in Mr. Jordan's mind that my brother was the Whitney's slave.

"Louisa," he said, "I cannot imagine how difficult it would be for you to find your brother and then deal with the fact that he is still a slave. I have a plan for that. I know Eli needs to use the Yale laboratory and needs the help of his teachers to make the cotton-cleaning machine practical. I will offer to buy his slave, because I need a good pressman. This will be a private matter between Mr. Whitney and me. I told them that I would not involve any of the groups that are working to get rid of slavery. I will also get the slave, possibly your brother, to work with Eli to make the mechanical cotton cleaner. When he is not helping Eli with the invention, he will have a job keeping the presses running at the newspaper. I think the Whitney family will be agreeable to this slave buying his freedom over the next seven years. I know Eli wants to make sure he gets help and that the slave does not give his idea to anyone else. So making a seven-year contract with the slave should take care of that. In reality, Louisa, the slave will be a free man, because I will pay him well for his work, and I will not accept any payment for his freedom. He will have to keep his seven-year commitment, but that time will go fast."

He went on, "Here is my proposal—and before you make a decision, I want you to know that if either or both of you oppose my plan, I understand. Providing the Whitney family agrees to my offer, I would like both of you to go to South Carolina to bring the slave back to Boston. Louisa, you will know right away if he is your brother. If he is your brother, then he should be willing to return with you. I suspect the two of you would have a lot to talk about. Of course, I expect my reward to be many good stories for the paper."

Mr. Jordan turned to Sam and said, "Sam, I picked you because you are not married, and you are so dedicated to this newspaper. I also know that you volunteered for the night watch and were part of the group that saved Louisa's life."

I interrupted Mr. Jordan, and said, "Sam, why didn't you tell me?"

Sam replied that he was so upset by the tea incident that it was just his way of making amends. Now, Mr. Jordan was confused, because he thought Sam was talking about dumping the tea in Boston Harbor. Both Sam and I said it was something personal, and we both would just like to forget it.

Mr. Jordan continued, "Sam, I want you to write about how Africans are treated in the South, compared to their treatment in Boston. Make note of the way Louisa is treated compared to your treatment. I also want you to protect Louisa, because the South is a dangerous place for black people, even if they are as well known as Louisa. Both of you should know that I have done my homework on this project, and there will be what I call 'safe homes' for you all along the way. Louisa, Alex and Sally can stay with us until you return. We would enjoy having your son as a guest. It has been a while since my wife and I got to enjoy a child in our home. Sally, I am sure, will have no trouble moving back for a couple of months. I will check your apartment daily on my way to or from work. Oh yes, you will have a private carriage for the entire trip, and the drivers will also be trained guards. I do not expect any trouble, but you will be well-protected in the unlikely event trouble happens. Louisa, if this young man is your brother, I have something very special to offer you. I do not want to talk about it now, but I promise you something will happen that even you could not have thought about if my hunch is correct and that slave is your brother."

Mr. Jordan finished by saying, "It is time to get back to work, unless either of you have questions."

Neither Sam nor I were prepared to ask Mr. Jordan anything. He had such a good plan that the only thing left to do was decide on accomplishing it or not. He told us that he did not want a decision until the next day. He said that he would drop by tomorrow at mid-morning, and we would talk more then. That night, right after supper, I told Sally and Alex about Mr. Jordan's offer. Alex made my decision easy when he said,

"Mother, you are going, aren't you?"

Sally was very supportive. She told me that Alex would indeed enjoy his time at the Jordan home, especially if the big tree house was still there. She would also keep check on the apartment, because she knew a man might not be as sharp-eyed as a woman. She laughed and said,

"Now aren't you happy you didn't get that dog the other day?"

Alex yelled, "Mom, you mean we can have a dog?" I told him that would be the first thing we would do when I got back home.

Sally said, "By the time you get home, Alex will have me reading the Bible on my own."

My decision was made.

On Imagination

Now here, now there, the roving fancy flies,
Till some lov'd object strikes her wand'ring eyes,
Whose silken fetters all the senses bind,
And soft captivity involves the mind.

Phillis Wheatley

Chapter 18—The Improbable Dream

Even though I was taken from my family at such an early age, they have always been a part of my life. In my thoughts and dreams, I see my family as if they were here and a part of my everyday existence. As I walk to work this morning, I am talking with my African family about the trip. I sense their approval and support. I also find myself wondering what else Mr. Jordan has in mind. He gave me a clue when he said that even I could not imagine it. The only thing I find unimaginable is being reunited with my brother.

Mr. Jordan's idea that my brother is in South Carolina cannot be right. The thought made him so happy that I played along with the idea. Then it occurred to me that we need to know what to do if the slave is not my brother. Does Mr. Jordan still want to buy him? I am sure the answer will be "yes" but I must check as soon as I see him.

I had been so deep in thought that it seemed as if I got to work without walking. Again, I was the first one to arrive. I sat down at my desk and started making a list of the things I needed to take with me. I had never been on a long trip in a carriage. I had heard people talking about how pleasant coaching is, with the better-sprung vehicles and the good road along the seacoast. If the truth be known, I found it difficult to think about a carriage going from Boston to Charles Towne. Riding around Boston in the best carriage on paved roads for any length of time left you feeling beat-up. How would I endure going a thousand miles in a coach?

Another problem bothered me. By my calculations, even in a speedy carriage, the most we could hope for is about 30 miles a day. At that rate, it would take us about 34 days to get to Charles Towne. Mr. Jordan kept saying we would be gone about two months, but it would take at least two months to make the round trip, and we would need to spend at least two weeks in Charles Towne before returning. I decided to stop all this fretting and get back to planning. Knowing Mr. Jordan, as soon as we agreed to his idea, we would start the next day, so I had better be ready.

I was very tense, because of both the job and the impending trip. The people around me sensed my discomfort and did their best not to bother me. You would think that with all the people coming and going in our busy room, I would not be so easily frightened. Then I looked up, and there stood Andrew. I was startled, and Andrew jumped as if he had been stung by a hornet. He apologized for scaring me, but I said,

"I think I should apologize to you, because you jumped like a scared rabbit."

He told me that he was actually trying not to bother me, because I was so deep in thought. I laughed and said,

"For someone trying not to bother me, you sure did a good job of doing just the opposite."

We were a playful bunch. Adam arrived next, and finally, Sam. Sam wasted no time in telling me that he was prepared to make the trip, and he hoped that I had come to the same decision. I told him that I did not hold out much hope for seeing my brother, but with just a glimmer of hope, I had to go.

Andrew said that Adam and he were eager to know what Mr. Jordan had planned for us. I said,

"Andrew, one thing I won't miss over the next few months is your silliness."

He knew I was teasing. I asked everybody to gather at the big table. After everyone was seated, I started telling them what happened yesterday. Sam added details that I left out. When we finished, both Andrew and Adam said that they could not believe we would be willing to ride that far in a carriage. Adam had made a carriage trip to New York, and he said his rear end still hurt. He added that the trip was made in a $25 carriage with no springs, but Mr. Jordan's carriage was expensive and was made for long trips. Adam said that it had taken him eight days to get from Boston to New York, but one of those days was spent in a small town—he could not remember the name—while a wheel and some other stuff was repaired. There was great concern by all of the men about my being able to endure such a hard trip. Yet, even more, they feared for my life going back into slave territory. Before the trip, the fact that I was an African woman and a former slave was not considered. I guess the column took all of their attention. Now, they were being forced to see the real me and the difficulty of being female and a former slave. This view of me made them uncomfortable.

Then I changed the conversation to the "Boston Report". I said that since we would not be together after that day, we needed to do some fast, long-range planning. There were enough columns written for the next six months, but we all agreed to make a list of twenty topics that would work in the "Boston Report". We thought it would be best not to write material too far in advance, because we wanted our column to be fresh and timely. It was understood that Andrew and Adam might need to keep the column going more or less on their own even after we returned. It was clear that Mr. Jordan wanted the special report well done, and that would take a lot of time. Both Andrew and Adam said they would have no trouble keeping the column running at a high level. They also said that they would involve us as much as possible so we would still feel a part of every column. I felt relieved, and then, deep inside me, I felt fear similar to the panic I felt in the little boat when I was torn from my family and mother Africa.

Just then Mr. Jordan arrived. I had to be careful because he had been so much a part of my life of late that I began to think of him more like a father than my boss, but he was all business today, and my feelings quickly changed from talking to a friend to listening to the boss. He very abruptly asked me for my decision, and I told him I would make the trip. He then turned to Sam, and before he could ask the question, Sam said, "I'm going." Mr. Jordan then said that the most difficult part was over. He thought it would be next to impossible to get vict.... He caught himself. He changed what was going to come out "victims" to volunteers and laughed as if he had made the mistake on purpose. I had to wonder about that little joke—if it was a joke.

However, he did play one big trick on us, and we all fell for it. Mr. Jordan could not hold back his laughter. There he sat at the head of the table, laughing so hard he could not keep his composure. On the other hand, we were sitting around the table, somewhat gloomy and overcome by the tasks before us for the next several months. By now, tears were coming from Mr. Jordan's eyes, and he was entirely bent over in laughter. Most of us thought his silly little joke about volunteering was not even a joke, but a mistake—a mistake that showed his true feelings. Even if it was a joke, it was not that funny, and we could not understand Mr. Jordan's reaction. Perhaps this was gallows humor of a sort that had the executioner laughing instead of—I chuckle as I write the word—the victim.

Mr. Jordan regained our attention as he took control of the meeting, but his little inside joke would not allow him to stop laughing. As he looked around at our faces, he burst back into the most uproarious laughter I have ever seen. I began to wonder when this would all stop. It was time for me to say something. I said,

"Mr. Jordan, sir, we cannot imagine what you find so funny. Is it the way we look, or are dressed, or something we said?"

Mr. Jordan replied with three polite ways of saying "No," but he was still so caught up with the humor of the situation known only to him that his answers forced through laughter were barely understandable. He apologized to us and took leave of the room to calm down. We sat there thinking perhaps we had just seen the owner of the newspaper go mad. We all began to feel sorry for a man under so much pressure and forgot about why we were sitting around the table in the first place.

When Mr. Jordan returned, he still seemed ready to explode in laughter, but was able to finally adjust. I said,

"Mr. Jordan, you must let us in on your little ruse. There is obviously something we don't know that you know."

He finally spoke so we could understand him. "Louisa, you are correct. I tricked the lot of you. Do you really believe that I would want you to ride a coach all the way to Charles Towne?" The words, "A ship" poured out of my mouth. There was a big sigh of relief from everyone sitting at the table.

"Why, sure," Mr. Jordan replied. "In a way, however, I put your loyalty to the test. It is interesting to me that none of you were concerned about your own comfort and safety. I assure you that I would not ask you to do something that I myself would not do, and there is no way I would ride in a carriage all the way to Charles Towne. Besides, I need you here at the newspaper instead of spending months of time traveling through the wilderness. As I said, I am not interested in a travelogue."

I got booking for you on the merchant ship Friendship. It worked out well, because she is making a voyage to pick up spices, sugar, and coffee, and will drop you off at the port of Charles Towne, and then pick you up on her way back. By the way, Louisa, they did ask me if you would be willing to recite some of your poetry during the trip. I told them that was up to you, but I suspect the price of the tickets were reduced in anticipation of your performing. Anyway, be prepared for the captain to ask that favor of you. Louisa will have a private berth, and the others will have good lodging in the guest quarters. Sam, I've been to your place, and I think you will find everything on board ship as good as you have at home. So, Sam and the two guards will have the guest quarters to themselves. On the way back, of course, the slave will use the guest quarters. Louisa and Sam, if I failed to tell you, I bought the slave, and you will bring him back with you."

He continued, "When you get to Charles Towne, you will stay at the Whitney plantation. You will have the use of a carriage and any other thing you might need. The ship leaves early tomorrow. You will be expected to board before dark. They want to show you important things on the ship before it gets dark. You can go home for the night and get back early, but it would be best, according to the captain, to spend tonight on board the ship. You have the rest of the day off, so there should be plenty of time to get your things together. Oh yes, Louisa, everything I said about Alex and Sally was true. Why don't you bring them over tonight, and then we will all be there in the morning to send you off?"

I told Mr. Jordan that, even though I expected things to happen fast, they were happening a little too fast for me. I was happy to have the time off to get ready, and I would talk with Sally to find out what she and Alex wanted to do. With that, I bade Andrew and Adam farewell and left immediately to get my things together and be with my family.

When I got home, Sally and Alex had just finished lunch. They were both very surprised to see me. They already knew I was going on a trip, but had no idea it would start tonight. Sally decided to wait until morning to make arrangements with Mr. Jordan for them to stay with the Jordan family until I returned. She said she would feel more comfortable talking with Mr. Jordan first. I told her I understood. She also said she wanted to help me and would be too tired to prepare the things for her and Alex. From my experience of going to England, I knew how to pack. I had just bought three leather bags that were just right for the trip. At the time I bought them, I had no idea I would be using them so soon. Then it occurred to me that I had not made financial arrangements for Sally and Alex. I had some money at the house, but most of it was in the bank, and neither Sally nor Alex could get to it.

Sally was just wonderful. She told me that she had plenty of money and not to worry. I showed her where I hid the money in the apartment, and she said that they probably would not need it. I did not want Sally to use her money, but I did not have time to deal with her stubbornness. In fact, even if I had the time, I doubt I could have changed her mind. I would take care of her financially as soon as I returned. Sam and a friend of his were going to pick me up. The friend had a carriage large enough to hold our entire luggage. I had neither stopped nor eaten since I got home. Six bells chimed, and I knew Sam would soon be there. Sally helped me get the bags to the front stoop, and then she insisted that I eat something. I did not realize how hungry I was until I sat down at the table. Sally had everything ready for me, which was good because Sam arrived just as I swallowed the last bite. This is no way to leave on such an important trip, but it worked as well as if we had planned for a month.

At this point, friends, my story has gone from recall to writing a journal. Writing is healing for me, so I doubt that I will ever stop. When I was mostly writing poetry for a living, I found writing prose relaxing. Thus, this book was started. Now, I am writing for the newspaper, and I want to spend what spare time I have writing poetry. However, with so much happening to me, I must share those events with others. If the person in Charles Towne is my brother, words must be written to tell about this most improbable event. Then there is Mr. Jordan's plan, a scheme that even I could not imagine. Surely, such a happening must be recorded. As you recall, if the slave is my brother, Mr. Jordan has a rather brilliant plan for us.

I must write about the beauty of open sea, but the ship often gets close to land, showing yet another type of beauty. The captain uses these stunning landscapes to help guide the ship during the day, so at night he used the stars, and during the day he used landmarks. Yes, another book is in order. For now, however, I am putting down my pen until we reach the Port of Charles Towne.

On the fifth night at sea, the Captain asked to meet with all the guests after supper. The trip was so fast and smooth it seemed as if we had just left, and yet we were only hours away from our destination. I must do some reading about sailing when I have the time. It amazes me how they maneuver the sails to catch the wind. Right now, I find myself wondering how they will reverse the process to go in the opposite direction on the return trip. Ironically, the meeting after supper was about sailing and how difficult it was for the Friendship to dock after entering the harbor. There will be other ships close by, and the harbor has little or no wind. Now, I know what the huge oars lining the sides of the ship are all about. The captain warned us that, depending on the tide, he might anchor in deep water, and we would take a small boat to shore. On the return trip, when the 'Friendship' is loaded with cargo, we will most certainly be brought on board using a small boat. He told us that he would be giving a lot of commands and occasionally might use words we find offensive. The Captain, in so many words, asked us to stay out of the way. He thanked me for the recital I gave last night and said he had never heard such fine poetry.

True to his word, being on a ship entering a port was an exciting experience. The decision was made to anchor in the deep water and row us into the dock. The captain thought that since that will be the way we get back on board, it would be good practice to leave that way today. There is no dignified way for a lady to climb down a rope ladder into a moving boat. All of the men did me the honor of looking toward shore as I made my descent. My heart was racing. It would take about an hour for our carriage to get to the plantation. When our little boat reached shore, there was a carriage waiting for us a stone's throw from the dock. I have a new-found respect for Mr. Jordan—as if he needed any more of my respect. He thought of everything. All I had to do was get my belongings together. My thoughts drifted to the chance of

Mr. Jordan's idea about my brother becoming a reality as the coach got closer to the plantation.

We pulled into a curved driveway leading up to a large, columned, white house. The outline of a man by a small outbuilding caught my attention. Instantly, I knew! I knew! Oh Lord, I knew! There was no doubt. I jumped off the moving coach screaming,
"Jololi! Jololi! Jololi!"
Words in our native language of Wolof flowed from my mouth as if I were still in my village trying to get my brother's attention. When the man turned and started running toward me, I knew for sure he was my brother, and he knew that I was his sister. I cannot imagine what must have been going through his mind. He had not been told a thing. Praise the Lord, for He is a mighty God!

Printed in the United States
69179LVS00001B/62